Acknowled[illegible]ents

I'd just like to say a big thanks to my editors, Kristen and Caityln for going through my book bit by bit.

Also my model on the front cover for letting us take so many pictures of you till we got the right one.

And thanks to everyone in my college class for letting me ramble on about my work.

www.fast-print.net/store.php

THE BLOOD SERIES: BLOOD WOLF

All characters are fictional.
Any similarity to any actual person is purely coincidental.

A catalogue record for this book is available from the British Library

ISBN 978-178456-159-8

First published 2015 by
FASTPRINT PUBLISHING
Peterborough, England.

BLOOD *Wolf*

1

Mon Cherie

She charged furiously towards the vampire, her arms outstretched to tackle him. A smile creased along his lips as he waited till the last minute to move to the side. The girl tried to stop herself from falling, but was knocked to the matt by a pillow hitting her back. Feathers followed her to the matt as muffled laughter assaulted her ears.

She pulled a feather from her mouth; she couldn`t believe she had agreed to this. *Why had she agreed to this with him?* Alexis tried to stop herself from being furious at Louie, seeing a smile creased along his face. Standing up and brushing herself off again, she soaking up the atmosphere of the old gym, trying to calm her frantically beating heart.

Louie could detect the racing pulse and an evil smile crossed his lips. Alexis caught this and bolted towards him clumsily.

Louie launched himself upward and landed on one of the ceiling beams and she crashed onto the matt for the millionth time that day. Snickering he looked down towards her "You are not even trying, Mon Cherie." Louie sounded amused, his hands placed on his hips and his head titled to the side.

Louie's French accent strongly pushed forward when he spoke. His dainty body was mostly all legs, standing at a 5ft 7 dwarfed by the interior of his surroundings. Louie Des Channel had light blonde hair that went down to his shoulders and his blue eyes were strikingly unusual. His colourful clothes did not suit his nature but showed his French heritage.

The girl pushed herself to her feet as the vampire returned to the ground in front of her. "I'm trying..." Her breath hitched as she took another blow to her stomach. She flinched as she waited for another to follow but none came. Her eyes were shut tight, her head curled into her chest. She lifted her head; she tried to show that she was strong...that she wanted to do this.

Forget the pain - she whispered in her own head. She wished it was that easy, it was all mind over matter. "I thought you were going to teach me how to fight, not beat me up" her voice was dry; she needed some fluids, fast. She felt weak, pushed over and like she was about to get another punch. She began to back away as the French male in front of her started to laugh, it was a pompous laugh. One she never enjoyed hearing from Louie.

Louie shook his head and moved towards her a step at a time as if trying to torment her, stalk her. He was as slippery as an eel.

"You asked me to teach you, so I am only doing as you asked Mon Cherie" Louie's voice was soaked with his accent, every word he said dripped with his French-ness. He was far too cocky for his own good as well.

Alexis was moving backwards as fast as she could without turning around or falling over, her eyes never left the French male in front of her. "I meant like an hour every few days. Not once every blue moon, so my bones are going to be killing me for the rest of my life" Alexis dramatically moved back a few more quick steps hoping he wouldn't notice.

Another laugh followed and another step...before her back hit into what felt like a brick wall. No heat came from it, and if she hadn't been thrown about for the last couple of hours and was already in pain. She was sure it would have been sore.

Louie stopped in his tracks and Alexis took that as a good sign, she tilted her head back to see Vladimir.

A deep sigh of relief came from her lips as she turned back to face Louie. "Have I interrupted something?" Vladimir's thick accent purred out around Alexis's ears although he was clearly directing the question towards Louie. Vladimir was always as busy as a bee; she was surprised he had found the time now to get here and save her.

Alexis had learned long ago that when Vladimir was speaking unless she was the only person in the room, then he wasn't talking to her. Vladimir trusted Alexis to be the easiest out of the two.

Louie was normally the one creating trouble – she often laughed when Vladimir joked about how much a distress his life has been since he had changed Louie into a vampire. Alexis was not in the least bit sure how the sire thing worked but as far as she knew – it had nothing to do with controlling each other. Louie couldn't ever do a thing Vladimir told him.

It was his goal in life.

As a vampire that life wasn't very short either. Vladimir was much taller than Louie; his hair was long also, but darker – almost black. His hair was much longer, stretching right down his back, completely split in a middle pattern.

Vladimir's eyes were the same as his hair; dark brown, in the dark it was like you couldn't see the white. Alexis's could definitely say, out of the two, Vladimir was more dangerous, and more deadly. Vladimir dressed more modern, a black shirt, with normally dark grey or navy blue trousers. He always seemed to be smartly dressed.

Louie still held the smirk on his face as he shook his head before answering with a dramatic laugh. "No of course not. We were just training. She wanted to learn how to fight. She definitely needs training after what I have seen. I do not suggest putting her into any dog fights anytime soon" A harsh hit, Alexis cringed at the word dog.

Normally Louie didn't do such a low blow. He was baiting her. She hated where she had come from. She didn't want anything to do with her heritage. Vladimir and Louie had told her enough to scare her out of that. They had discussed the many things that her '*breed*' had done.

They were dangerous and that was why she knew it was a great decision to suppress the werewolf inside of her. It was not getting out, Alexis was making sure of that. She didn't want to know anything about her werewolf side, she wanted it gone.

Now.

It had done her no good so far, after all she had been living with vampires and there was no need for the werewolf gene. She sometimes wondered if the werewolves could ever be so dangerous, but she had also seen what a werewolf could do to vampires. Vladimir had brought in a women, a women with her face marked with scratches – she was scared for eternity due to how dangerous her kind were. She didn't want to be counted in with her *'kind'*.

She was glad that Vladimir had raised her, even if she was stuck in a house with Louie as well. "I would be better if you actually taught me and didn't hit me all the time" Alexis threw back feeling a lot stronger now that Vladimir was here, she felt more protected and grounded.

Although she still held back against him, she wasn't about to give Louie another opening to fling her across the room. She knew he would take that chance. Her back was already aching from being thrown against the wall; Vladimir was never going to get that picture back now. It was smashed. "You don't learn unless I hit you. You understand that you learn by doing, Mon Cherie" Louie shoved his hands in his pockets and leaned back on his feet.

He was clearly enjoying every minute of this. Alexis turned her head to look at Vladimir and he shrugged his shoulders towards her. He obviously couldn't see a problem with any of this. She switched her gaze between the two of them waiting for at least one of them to do anything.

That didn't seem to be happening. She threw her hands up in the air dramatically and stormed out the room, a laugh echoed behind her and she knew exactly who it was; Louie's.

She hated him sometimes.

2

Permission bites

Alexis began to change as soon as she got into her room; bouncing the door closed with her foot behind her she jumped out of her sweaty clothes, flinging them beside the door of the bathroom and dived into her warm shower.

It felt great against her skin and all at once seemed to ease away the pain she had just endured from Louie, the French vampire. She shook her head off from those thoughts and focused on relaxing in the shower. She couldn't stand to be smelly especially when she was around vampires who had a heightened sense of smell.

Louie always liked to point out if there was a smell coming from her, normally as dramatically as possible. It was always embarrassing and childlike. But then again Louie seemed to be stuck at a very immature age. She wasn't sure if that were a good thing or a bad thing.

He couldn't have been much older than her; maybe about 24 years old? Yeah, well that was what age he looked. His real age was 136. Although it was hard to believe someone that old could ever be THAT immature. But no one had ever spent a few bored hours with Louie.

He was the brother she never wanted or the crazy uncle she wished she could get away from. He was harmless of course and in his own weird way he was part of her family and if she were honest she would miss him if he wasn't around.

Within a few moments, Alexis's troubles began to wash away and as she washed out the conditioner feeling already more at ease. It was like her troubles were just washing away with the water.

Stepping out of the shower, squeezing the water out of her hair and grabbing a towel she wrapped it around her body and walked out of the bathroom to find Vladimir looking around her room. He seemed to be fixated on one of her pictures, one of a fairy surrounded by taller mushrooms and wildlife.

A favourite of hers, one that Vladimir seemed to be studying intently. She stood for a moment thinking *'At least it isn't Louie; otherwise coming out in a towel was a bad idea'*. Alexis had a much stronger bond with Vladimir, he was like a father figure towards her, never seeing her as anything more than a child in his life. Whereas Louie was more like the creepy uncle who would flirt with anyone and anything that was around even Alexis. She always tried to avoid being alone with him, if she could help it.

The older Alexis got, the more Louie seemed to become more interested in talking to her and flirting with her. He always joked that it was all fun and games but that was somewhere that Alexis would rather stay away from.

So in that sense, Vlady was safer territory for her. A smile moved along Alexis's face and she couldn't help but move forward into the room knowing she was in safe hands. "How can I help you Vlady?" Alexis beamed out towards Vladimir; turning towards her, the older vampire shook his head at her old nickname for him.

Although he never really said much about it, a little smile always let Alexis now that he was happy hearing her call him that, even if he wouldn't admit it. "I just wanted to inform you that we were having a meeting tonight and there would be some other visitors about the house. I would like you to stay in your room if that is at all possible, Alexandra"

Now this was serious, Alexis could tell. Vladimir never used her full name unless he meant it. His stern, worried father look told Alexis that he was only looking out for her and that he was being serious about who was coming tonight. He didn't want her near them or in most cases – he didn't want them anywhere near her.

More often than not it was vampires that came into this house and Vladimir liked to make sure that Alexis didn't become a new edition with a bite mark. Which Alexis could completely agree on. She never saw the excitement in having someone bite you.

The thought of it always made her face tense up in disgust. Although this spiked Alexis's interest; she hadn't met too many people and any new additions in the house she often liked to poke her nose in and see what was happening. But with the way Vladimir was acting she doubted this was the time to start being nosy. She also knew this was the time to talk about something else.

Something she had been thinking about for a long while. If he was going to be busy tonight, then his mind was probably on a lot of other things, which meant – to Alexis- there was more likely for him to say yes. Alexis took in a deep breath and Vladimir raised his eyebrows in question, anticipating that she already wanted to say something. Alexis's cheeks flared red and she smiled. "Ok. I promise not to go out and wander tonight. But

I do want to ask you one thing...." She trailed off casting her eyes up to his as if looking for acknowledgement that she could ask a question.

After a few moments of Vladimir saying nothing, Alexis continued. "I want to go to a real school. Just for my last year. I know I'm ready and I know you guys don't like me leaving the house. There's a school just a few blocks away from here. They have lunch breaks where I could check in and you gave me a phone that I don't use, this could be what I use it for. But I need something to do. I need to see what's out there. It's not like it's going to drag me away from you guys. We're immortal. It's kinda hard to fit in somewhere when you don't age like everyone else does. I know I have asked this before and I know your answer was no to ensure my safety but I am sure you could check out the school and always keep tabs on it. I am not going to be there all the time, there are lots of holidays and it's only just for the last year?" ending her rant with a question, Alexis let her words hang in the air as she looked over Vladimir and tried to determine what he was going to say.

She couldn't believe she had said so much. She had only meant to ask him a question and she had turned it into a speech.

A long speech. *Who was she trying to convince here? Herself or Vladimir?* Alexis was nervous of this more than she had ever been before but she knew it was right, she had been out of the world for too long. There had to be something she could learn in school that she couldn't do here. There had to be something she was missing out on.

After all not everyone was home schooled. She didn't think anyone else was home schooled actually. She felt at a lost, she was scared about doing something new and leaving her family even if it was just for a few hours at a time.

Then again at the same time she wanted to be free for once, she wanted to express herself, to see what life was like outside of her nest. She wanted to spread her wings and see if she could take off by herself. She didn't want to keep relying on Louie and Vladimir for everything.

As much as she didn't want to leave them she knew that she couldn't stay looked up by their side forever, she wanted to be able to venture out on her own, she wanted them to be able to trust her too. He didn't seem surprised by this request but then again Alexis was getting older and he must have expected sooner or later that she would want to experience something else other than this house. He didn't give anything away; his face was blank of emotion as he thought about it. His eyes were piercing through her as if they couldn't even see her. His skin was always white as a sheet compared to his darker clothes.

Alexis almost sighed in defeat before he let out a breath. Alexis perked up. "I understand" Vladimir was serious and Alexis was sure his lips hadn't moved but she had heard the words. *Two words? That was all he was going to say?* Alexis couldn't even work out what those two words meant. *Did they mean yes? Was that a no?* She waited for more but Vladimir just looked at her blankly as if this was all he was going to say. She moved over to her wardrobe and started to take out her PJ's, when she turned back around Vladimir was gone.

There was no site or sound of him. She didn't even hear the door close on his way out. Alexis let out a deep sigh and sat on the bed. *Was she ever going to experience a real life?* She felt like a dangerous, caged animal being locked up here all the time.

Then again maybe that was how they saw her. She was after all a werewolf. The vampires she resided with never spoke highly of her species. *Did that mean they didn't trust her? Was that why they kept her so locked up? How could she have expected anything more than this?* She shook her head away from those bad thoughts. Vladimir would never treat her like that; she was nothing like her kind. She had made sure of that. She hadn't ever let that beast out of her head.

Alexis changed and crawled into bed, hoping that it would settle her erratic thoughts.

3

Not a spoil

"How can this even be acceptable?" Elizabeth spoke with a formal British accent, her beady eyes moved over to Vladimir with a smile.

Contradicting what she was saying. Elizabeth spoke up with grace and elegance that could never have been seen in the new century. She was something of a mystery to most people – it was like she had not adapted with the times and merely let herself stay frozen in her own time. She was a short brunette women; her eyes were green and she had curves in all the right places, sometimes more than in the right places and was always followed around by her puppy dog vampire; Katriss Johnston -

the most recent of her sired children. Katriss was quiet behind her like always.

Never bothering to interrupt, she wanted to please Elizabeth after all and right now that meant *'Don't speak unless spoken too'*. Katriss was a good pet and at this moment Elizabeth's favourite, she had many sired children and many favourites, but like any immortal she got bored over time and needed to have something with a little spice in her life.

"We can hardly force the pup to change; we wouldn't want her to turn against us after all this time. Besides there is no way to force a werewolf to change if they simple refuse to" Daniel was firm but kind with his words.

With Elizabeth, he was an elder of the vampire species; one of the oldest left and directing his species into a new age. Daniel had a rugged handsomeness about him; his short blonde was well cut and slightly spiked up. He wore lose clothes, mostly white and well cut, his suit was clean and as if it had been finely pressed. He had a formal attitude to him, he held himself with pride and loyalty.

Vladimir had an undying respect for his sire and how to keep the vampires in check. He had spent countless numbers of years by Daniel's side. He trusted him in this world like no other. "She has been working fine with Louie, training how to fight. We can't help that she has decided to supress her werewolf gene" Vladimir counted back; he kept his arms straight by his side as if he were being interrogated.

Although the room was full of vampires, Vladimir and Louie seemed to be the odd ones out. They were in the middle of the circle. The three elders stood in front of the two of the household and then around the circle were people they had sired or people that guarded them.

It was a mean looking bunch. Louie's attitude had dulled, his stance was nervous and his cocky, normal approach to everyone was missing just because of this *'new'* company.

Daniel seemed to consider what Vladimir was saying, a smile was never on his face but neither was a frown. He was very serious. The last elder Leonardo spoke forward. "We thought that was being sorted" his southern twang hung back on his words. He was from Texas, you could tell that even if you hadn't heard him speak. His cowboy image had never been lost over the years.

Leo still supported his cowboy hat and shoes, his trousers were topped with a horn belt, his shirt was stripped and then to top it off, his waist coat was covered with horses on the pockets to add effect.

Vladimir shook his head, he was more confident around the elders than Louie could be. He had been sired from Daniel after all, which was why he always spoke directly to him. He thought it would be easier. Elizabeth could see him as nothing more than a play toy and Leonardo never spoke much too him. Vladimir wasn't sure how Leonardo felt about him and right now it didn't matter. He didn't want Elizabeth's or Leonardo's approval.

"As I spoke last time, we have been trying to get the wolf out. Louie has been tormenting her to see if anger will even bring it out. But she feels that the wolf is dangerous. The background we decided to spin on her werewolf breed has scared her enough, the wolf in her may be lost forever. Is there any point in this?"

He cared for Alexis in many ways and he wanted to protect her from the elders but at the same time he knew he had done wrong by her, he had scared her from being who she really was.

The werewolf was supposed to be part of her and now it was nowhere to be seen. Leonardo smirked, gripping on to his trousers he swung his waist forward as if letting people know he wanted to talk. “You never lose the wolf. Believe me I have seen it happen. She’ll get the wolf back she just needs the right persuasion. Y’all just doing the wrong thing. She doesn’t need any more love and affection from the father she wished she had. She needs teachers and someone in charge. She was put in the wrong hands maybe it’s time someone took over from the young one” Leo’s words were not directed towards Vladimir even though his eyes casted over him.

Louie was in the background itching to talk. He was never one for being quiet and he wanted to voice his opinion, after all he was quite attached to the young wolf as well. He didn’t want to lose her because they weren’t right for the job. He was sure he could try harder. Daniel cocked his head towards his fellow elder and raised his eyebrows. “We want the young girl to be our guard not your spoil Leo” the Elder answered with a joking tone, but the seriousness was shown through his eyes. This had been the reason none of the elders had been left to raise the young wolf.

They knew that Elizabeth and Leonardo would only treat her as a play thing and there was more than likely a risk of being killed in their care if she spoke the wrong word.

They were vampires and she was a werewolf, they were natural born enemies.

Daniel knew she was a normal teenage girl as well as a werewolf and there was, of course going to be some disobedience. That was why this job was given to someone he trusted, someone with a little more feeling.

Vladimir had more years on him that he ever cared to admit and Daniel had spent many years trusting and relying on him. He was the clear choice. Daniel knew himself he couldn’t be entrusted with it either, he had too many people around him and he had to take care of new vampires, they couldn't very well put a werewolf girl with a beating heart in front of them.

That was too much of a temptation; she wouldn't have survived a week. "We need some improvements though…." Daniel's words held up and for the first time since they had entered the house he smiled. His ears perked open and his head tilted towards the ceiling of the house, he heard the small footsteps of someone moving through the house. Around the same time everyone else could hear it as well.

Vladimir held back a curse. Louie looked up in astonishment. "I see someone is awake" Daniel answered turning his eyes back towards Vladimir.

His look was one of curiosity and intrigued for two very good reasons; one of which was Vladimir's reaction to the girl being up in the care of so many vampires. The other was what the young girl was like now- he hadn't seen her since they had checked up on her on her tenth birthday.

That was quite a few many years ago now. She had been cute as a young pup and he was sure that would only grow with time.

“I’ll see what she wants and keep her away....” Louie spoke up for the first time, backing away slightly ready to leave the circle if he was told in a second that he could, he didn’t want to be here anymore than Vladimir did; probably more so and Vladimir answered that with a dirty look.

That was not something he should have said. He should have kept his mouth shut and Louie knew that. Elizabeth laughed at the young vampire speaking and Vladimir’s stare. She knew nothing like that would ever happen to her. She only kept and trained people who would obey her, the rest died - without a second thought. She was never one to give mercy.

Not that Leonardo or Daniel were very much different. None of them tolerated disobedience. “That will be all right Louis...”

“Louie” The young vampire interrupted. Daniel was surprised enough that he had built up the courage to even speak well enough answer him back. “Yes. I think Caleb can handle this. Would you mind?” Daniel’s eyes cast over the circle towards a young boy roughly a few years older than Alexis. His emo style brunette hairdo covered his forehead and stretched around his head like an uneven hat. His blue eyes stood out as big round circles, and his high cheek bones made him look like any teenage heart throb. His lips moved up at one side as his head nodded before he disappeared from the room without any spoken words.

Vladimir watched all of this with a fear of what might happen before turning back towards Daniel when the vampire was gone. “Are you sure that is wise? To her, he is a stranger in her house” Vladimir tried to reason with his sire but he could already see there was no use. This was what Daniel wanted and what Daniel wanted -he got. He was the most reasonable out of the three elders but he was still not use to not getting what he wanted.

Daniel was patient after all. “Exactly! I think it’s a magnificent idea. Caleb is a torment, worse than Louie I am sure. I have lived with him for long enough, he will break her. Besides it will give you a break from the life of looking after her” Daniel spoke with authority that was not to be broken. Vladimir sighed not knowing what else to say. He nodded his head and shot Louie a look, making sure that again – he wasn’t going to cut in. Daniel knew he had won before he even spoke and he knew that Caleb was the right person to get the wolf out of her.

It was also a chance for him to prove himself. Caleb was a child of Daniel's line and he was happy to have someone with powers beside him now. It wasn't a hard decision to make him a vampire; after all he needed someone with potential to follow his orders. Daniel felt like he needed someone that could be Loyal and obedient around him, someone who had some sort of special ability that Elizabeth couldn't tempt and that Leonardo couldn't threaten if things came to the worst.

Not that Daniel would ever let situations get that far. Vladimir looked around the room for a moment and then gazed towards the door, he wanted to check on Alexis and he wanted to see where she was and how she was going to react to Caleb.

"May I?" Vladimir asked Daniel directly and the smile that spread along Daniel's face was of no surprise. It was priceless. It was like a child who had a new present to open at Christmas. Daniel held his hand out towards the door "Please." Vladimir didn't need to be told twice; he flew out of the room and followed the sound of voices.

He didn't want Caleb to spend any more time with Alexis than he had to. He knew exactly where they were.

4

Typical temptation

Alexis tip toed along the floor as she headed for the kitchen, she knew she wasn't supposed to be out of her room at this time of night, especially not tonight; when Vladimir had asked her specifically not to. But she had forgotten the most important thing, to drink after exercising.

Alexis had been in that work out room for a long time and she had had hardly anything to drink while doing that and then she had proceeded to her bedroom where Vladimir had told her to stay in her room. She had fallen asleep shortly after that and now woke with a dying thirst. She didn't want to disobey

Vladimir, which was why she was trying to be quiet and take the long way down to the kitchen.

Although she didn't know if that would work considering they had hearing like a bat.

Vladimir always seemed to know where she was and what she was doing. She couldn't help that she needed a drink and that was exactly what she would tell him. She took in a deep breath and pushed on the right door knowing that it was the one to not squeak. She didn't want to attract unwanted attention. She avoided turning on the light and moved towards the fridge where she knew there was a cool refreshing drink for exactly this situation. She opened up the fridge and cringed at the site of the blood bags stacked in the fridge. She felt herself go green, bile raised in her throat and she swallowed it back "Wrong Fridge" She mumbled towards herself, she always seemed to do that. *Why couldn't she learn?* She shut the fridge door carefully trying to keep quiet and moved to the next fridge, smiling when she opened it to find her juice.

The exact thing she was craving. She opened the cap and drunk from it straight away, cleaning away all the dryness in her throat.

A sigh of relief left her throat when she stopped drinking and she took a step back giving her space to shut the door. "That seemed….." a smile echoed in his throat "…Enjoyable" Caleb couldn't help but grin as he leaned against the blood-filled fridge. Alexis's eyes widened and when he spoke, she automatically moved backwards. Her eyes scanned the room searching for someone she knew, someone she could talk to. She didn't know who this was. *Was this who Vladimir wanted her away from?*

She swallowed the lump in her throat. "Nothing to say young pup?" Caleb tilted his head and folded his arms in front of him as Alexis stared towards him. She gathered up her courage and pushed her chest out. She wasn't going to be insulted by anyone and she wasn't going to take to being called pup by someone who looked the same age as her. *Besides what had Louie once told her? 'If you act courageous most people won't be able to tell the difference'.* Alexis guessed this was time to test that theory.

After all this was her home, not his. “Who are you?” She tried to sound much stronger than she felt and she gripped her bottle of juice much tighter in her hand, hoping that it would show more strength. She remember Vladimir telling her that the little things you did with vampires mattered and if this was a vampire then she better test out the theory too. She tried to force herself to look serious and furrowed her brows in an attempt to seem un-amused with her guest.

Caleb pushed himself off the fridge and moved towards Alexis. “Cute. Acting like the guard dog already. I honestly don’t see what the problem is here.” Caleb took another slow two steps forward while he was talking. The room was dark and with the fridge shut, Alexis was struggling to keep her eyes focused on the dark, especially since Caleb was completely dressed in black. She could hardly make him out, luckily his pale complexion gave some clues as to where he was, since his hair was pitch black as well and it curved along his head, flowing over his forehead cascading and over his ears. Alexis stumbled back slightly until her back hit the worktops and she started to edge along them slightly.

"You don't scare me." she tried to keep her words steady and her face serious. She wasn't going to be scared off by some newbie in her house no matter what he was. Louie had said some vampires bark was worse than their bite; it was the quiet ones you had to watch out for.

Well this '*vampire*' didn't seem to be quiet, although Alexis didn't want to push her luck. After all Vladimir had just told her not to mess with any species unless she was sure of what they were. Alexis was only guessing that this boy was a vampire. *What else could he be?* He was in a home full of vampires - apart from herself.

Normally the visitors that came here were vampires. She had only ever seen one witch here and she was sure Vladimir had tried to make sure she hadn't seen that. *What she didn't see couldn't hurt her;* Vladimir often remarked. She laughed at the thought of it. "Really?" Caleb concurred as he took another soft step towards her, his feet never made a sound against the ground where as hers seemed more clumsy and even when she tiptoed she seemed to be more heavy footed. Alexis held her ground now, knowing that if she kept backing up then she would contradict what she was saying.

"Really" This seemed like more of a stand-off. *Who would give in first?* Caleb's smile was like a snake wrapping around her as he stood still for a moment before moving another step closer to her. When she didn't match his step, his eyebrows raised and his eyes showed all the amusement he felt. Another step forward put him within reaching distance of the young girl but she still held fast. "Funny…your body says different, your smell tells me your afraid." So he was a vampire then, since she knew the only ones that could smell your fear were vampires and werewolves – that she knew of. Vladimir would never let another werewolf into his house.

They were too dangerous. This only left him with one option. Vampire.

"Yet your holding your ground." a small chuckle came from the handsome vampires throat as he moved a little bit closer to her and as he expected, she didn't move back. "That could either be incredibly stupid or suicidal" Alexis swallowed the salvia that had risen into her mouth, showing how nervous she was at this moment. She doubted what Louie had said now. *Wouldn't he have backed down by now?* Her hands rose into fists beside her and Caleb's eyes scanned up and down her before looking back up to her eyes. "I bet you taste good." Alexis's mouth almost dropped open with those words; he couldn't possibly be thinking about biting her *...could he?*

He wasn't aloud. *Was he?* Vladimir had always said in his care no one would ever bite her. Alexis tried to think of something to say, stumbling over words in her head but nothing she could think of would come out. Caleb took in a deep breath and closed his eyes; his tongue snaked out and licked the top of his lips before opening his eyes to stare at Alexis's stunned face. *He wasn't going to do this was he? Right now?* "Hello Vladimir" Caleb spoke loud although kept his eyes towards Alexis. Alexis flinched and turned around to find Vladimir who was standing at the door staring at Caleb. His eyes were wide and he looked unfocused, it wasn't like anything Alexis had ever seen him be like. "Caleb" his eyes finally moved away from Alexis to stare at Vladimir. She looked between the two before moving away from Caleb slightly.

She didn't at all feel safe with him here. Not after everything he had said. There was something just not quite right about him. "I think it is time you returned to your room Alexandra"

Oh- Alexis held her tongue knowing that she shouldn't say anything at this point, knowing she couldn't say anything at this point. Vladimir didn't move his eyes to look at Alexis once; his eyes just stared towards Caleb assessing him.

Caleb seemed more laid back now, his hands dug in his pockets and his cheeky smile was playful. The complete opposite of Vladimir. Alexis began to move towards Vladimir ready to slip out of the room and head back up to her room apart from the fact Vladimir was standing in the way of the door. She looked up towards him, waiting for him to move and after a moment he slid to the side, still not looking towards her. She let out a deep sigh and walked towards her bedroom. "See you later, Alexandra" Caleb's voice trailed after her as she moved a little bit quicker towards her room, using the name Vladimir had used for her. She should never have left her room. She should have just gotten some water from the tap in her room.

Alexis rushed into her room and shut the door behind her, letting the air out of her lungs as she did. It felt like she had been holding her breath since she left that room. Shaking her head Alexis walked towards her bed and tried to snuggle back down to sleep.

Within moments Caleb and Vladimir had left the kitchen and returned back to the sitting room. "Interesting" Elizabeth mused when the boys returned to the circle, Vladimir re-joined Louie in the middle and Caleb added to the missing place in the circle. Daniel stayed quiet for a moment looking at his children before resulting in a smile. "I believe it is our time to depart. It's be an intriguing night. Caleb enjoy yourself here with Vladimir, I am sure he will be able to accommodate you with everything you will need, as for what the young wolf wants Vladimir – let her have her fun, the real world will more than likely drive her back towards us" Vladimir half smiled towards his sire, not a conversation he wanted to have with anyone.

Alexis of course wanted to experience life and Vladimir had been contemplating bringing it up to Daniel but of course with his '*abilities*', Vladimir should have guessed the vampire would have taken it on himself. Vladimir nodded his head once and Daniel left the room with most of his vampires.

Caleb and Louie stayed still in the room the same as Elizabeth. Elizabeth moved towards Vladimir, her eyes looked him over before she moved her mouth towards his ear. "Be careful, Vlad. You wouldn't want to get too close to the pup. People might get the wrong idea and think you care for her" her whisper moved against him and he refused to answer or move when she was this close. Elizabeth smiled and moved back from him before following Daniel and Leonardo out of the room; Katriss following close behind her. *That was unfortunate.*

Vladimir let out an un-needed breath before turning around to face Louie and Caleb. "Louie. Show Caleb to a room over in the west side of the house" He wanted him as far away from Alexis's room as possible.

It was going to be hard enough getting him to stay away from her while she was awake never mind while they were supposed to be sleeping. With that Vladimir left the room and retired to his study - away from the problems that had just been created for him.

5

That’s going to hurt in the morning

Alexis found herself moving though the house. There didn’t seem to be anybody about, she had been awake for an hour now. This was the first time living here that she had woke up to nobody answering her.

Normally she could hear Louie and Vladimir in another heated argument about something stupid, or they were over hungry and you could find them in the kitchen. That wasn’t the case. Alexis found herself trailing through the house looking for anybody “Hello…” Her voice echoed and she looked up, she had never really studied her home before, she had always been too busy with something else.

"Vladimir?" Alexis called out ducking into another room that she hoped might give her some luck as to where her careers were. "Louie?" *Now when had she ever shouted for Louie?* Normally she was shouting to get away from him, not for him to come to her. But still there seemed to be no answer.

Not a sound, or anything. This wasn't normal. It just wasn't right.

She found herself venturing into the gym – a male was moving around the room quickly, quicker than she had ever seen before. It wasn't Louie and it certainly wasn't Vladimir. He flipped over and moved into some fighting poses, fighting an invisible foe.

Alexis was fascinated, *who was this person, what was he doing?* She had never seen anyone move with so much precision, he seemed to have an elegance that she had never seen in anyone before. Her head tilted to the side self-consciously; her mouth opened slightly and her eyes widened, her heart skipped a heat beat before he opened his own mouth to speak. “You know it’s rude to stare” His back was turned, his t-shirt was soaked in sweat…but she recognised that voice, after all it wasn’t that long since she had heard it. Her eyes rolled as she spoke his name

“Caleb” *Why had he stayed? Was she stuck with just him? This could not be hell?* Questions circled around in her head so many that she didn’t know the answer too but she knew that one person could answer them. Caleb. A frown hit her lips before she placed her hands on to her hips and stood her ground. “Where’s Vladimir and Louie?” She was going to stick to getting answers and ignore everything else. She wasn’t going to let him bully her into anything else.

Caleb turned around for the first time and faced the young werewolf, his smile still evident on his face. The room was bright even with the curtains closed; the lights streamed overhead illuminating the place. The place was decorated with vibrating red colours – that was why this was her favourite place in the house. She loved the way the patterns around the room’s coven added to the old fashioned style of the house; the red's made it look rich and comfortable. It made it more like her home.

This was where Alexis would normally sit to read her books, study, or anything else she could get away with. It was a place she loved, undoubtedly. "Away" Caleb moved to the side of the room, as if no other reason was needed for the vampire's whereabouts. She raised her eyebrows as if waiting for more of an answer from him…but nothing came.

He didn't seem to want to give any extra information. She couldn't remember a time where Vladimir and Louie had both disappeared at the same time and especially not without letting her know. It was something new and something she definitely didn't like. She threw her hands up in the air and made a frustrated sound of annoyance.

A chuckle came from the young vampire and Alexis shot him an annoyed look. She turned around to march away but was stopped by his voice. "Stay. Please. A little birdy told me you wanted to learn how to fight. I can teach you… if you want?"

The question hung in the air like a bad smell and Alexis fought the urge to refuse the offer but this was what she needed, this was what she wanted. Someone to teach her how to fight, properly and not to put her on her ass like Louie seemed to enjoy doing. *Then again how did she know that Caleb wouldn't do the same*? She turned around to face him – hoping to judge why he wanted to do this. By the look on his face he seemed sincere, like he wanted to teach her.

She pursed her lips for a moment hoping it would help her make the decision before she bounced her head in to a sharp nod. "Fine." She wasn't sure what else to say, she wanted to come back with some smart aleck remark but couldn't find the right words to do so. She didn't even want to try. She moved to the side and stripped off her jumper getting ready to fight or learn to fight him anyway. She turned to face him awaiting some sort of instruction.

Caleb's smile for the first time seemed one of genuine amusement, he moved himself to the middle of the gym where four mats had been placed to make a square and he waved his hand offering Alexis to join him. She did. “Do you know any sort of defensive stance or ways to protect yourself?” his question seemed light hearted and one of actual intrigue, which made Alexis reply more sheepishly with the shake of her head.

“Then I guess that will be where we start then” Caleb began to move himself into a defensive stance explaining exactly what he was doing and how he was doing it. “The most stable shape in the world is a pyramid. You need to move your body in to this position…” He demonstrated, his eyes focusing on her and once he was in the position he signalled her to copy him. “…Your feet have to be wide apart, the more surface area you have the harder it will be to knock you over. Move your leading leg forward slightly ready to counter act any move that is pushed to you” A smile curved his lips when Alexis seemed to find difficult doing this; she seemed to be all tangled up. Her eyebrows bunched up into the middle as she tried to copy what he was doing.

Caleb moved closer to her and kicked her feet wider apart “Flatten your feet, use your full bodies weight to your advantage" he asked for her hand and she trustingly gave it to him, with that he pulled her leading leg towards him slightly getting her into her defensive stance. "That's it. Easier than you think" Alexis looked towards him trying to copy what he was saying, she felt balanced more in this position although she failed to see how this would help her in any way.

In this position she felt more exposed. "How is this supposed to help me?" She questioned looking down at herself before moving back up towards him. Caleb began to circle her and she tried to stay in the centre position with her eyes following him but her eyes couldn't follow him all the way round.

Back around to the front he came and then before she knew it he moved to push her off balance. Alexis squeezed her eyes shut tightly, knowing this was when Louie would normally send her flying. But she didn't move, she felt the *'dunt'* of his hands against her chest and the wind move out of her body but she didn't fly back, she barely even moved from the position she was in. She just rocked slightly.

Alexis stared at Caleb amazed. “That is how it is meant to help you. Now let’s practice landing properly from fights” Caleb turned his back on her and moved to the other side of the mat. “Landing? What do you mean land properly?” Alexis moved out of the pyramid position and she felt her thighs begin to ache. She guessed the stable position was just a little bit too much for her body since she had never moved her body into that position before. She tried to stretch it off and moved closer to Caleb. He shook his head, a smile moving over his features once more. “Well unfortunately you’re going to end up on your back at some point in a fight. It’s better to know how to land so you’re not going to break something and you may just hurt yourself a little” Caleb explained moving towards Alexis and grabbing her, she gasped.

“Now when I trip you up roll your back, let yourself fall and don’t fight it. Stretch your arm out to your side and hit the mat, it’ll make the noise that you’re supposed to make when you hit the ground hard. It’ll distract the attacker” without another word,

Caleb did what he said he was going to do and tripped her to the ground.

Alexis forgot to roll her back and move her arm and landed with a thud, which hurt. She let out a cry and Caleb flinched, yanking her back off the ground. "Roll Dammit. I said roll and let yourself fall" Caleb growled towards her, his face screwing up as he spoke to her.

Alexis nodded her head "Sorry forgot that part" Caleb shook his head, *why did he even care if he hurt this girl?* He was just training her to be a guard dog and pushing her to change. That was his task but yet when she let out that cry it had echoed through him like nothing he had ever felt. He pushed it off and tried to avoid the thought moving Alexis into the same position. "Try again" A few more times Caleb and Alexis practiced the rolls before he moved on to other basic defensive techniques, he taught her how to counteract a blow to the stomach or the face. He'd almost taken her head clean off without thinking about it.

Which was bad on his part.

It didn't seem to faze her, she flinched a few times and he was sure there was going to be bruises all over her body considering the amount of times she had failed to block him or failed to land properly.

After a couple of hours of practicing; Alexis was beginning to get the hang of it. She was beginning to understand how to land properly, creating a big noise without hurting herself. She managed to block the most of Caleb's blows, part of her knew that he had lightened up and that if really wanted to, he could have taken her down without a second thought.

That didn't seem to bother Alexis nearly as much as it should. She was happy that she was actually getting to learn something; Louie would have been a great teacher if he had taught her something instead of showing her he could fling her across a room. Equally she was sure she had earned the same amount of bruises but this time they didn't seem to hurt as much – she felt like she had them for a reason.

Caleb had stopped his blows and used his speed to move behind her once more, slowly beginning to trip her up and when she landed it without any trouble he couldn't help but smile. "I think you got it." Caleb smirked and moved away to the side where his towel was sitting as well as a shirt and jeans. He didn't even begin to put them on considering how much he had begun to sweat, he had more trouble holding back from using his full strength on her than he had had on the work out beforehand.

He needed a shower to cool himself off and clean himself up. He also felt like he needed to get his head back in the game, he was supposed to be antagonising her – he was supposed to be pushing her to the edge so that she would turn into the wolf inside herself.

Alexis moved herself up on her elbows in curiosity, a smile on her face. Caleb may have been an ass to her last night but he had made it up to her today – that and he hadn't answered her questions about Vladimir or Louie. But that didn't seem to matter when he had taught her how to fight – well taught her how to take a couple of blows and how to fall.

“Thank you” Alexis managed to say before Caleb was moving away out the door without even a word of goodbye. Alexis lay back down staring up at the ceiling, her bones screaming out to be healed. She gently moved herself to her feet as her thighs began to protest, she worked against the pain and moved back to the door where she had left her jumper. She moved out of the room and back to her room, temporarily forgetting about her missing guardians and retiring back for a well needed shower and rest.

6

Bane of my existence

"Can we not just go out?" Louie whispered turning from the door and moving towards the table Vladimir had taken to residing at. They were in Vladimir's second office and he had locked the door so Louie wasn't able to go out to Alexis's shouting for them.

This was under agreement; Daniel had told them to let Caleb do his *'thing'*.

Vladimir was not at all pleased at ignoring her shouts for them and he could tell Louie wasn't either. Louie had continuously tried to make noise – indicating to Alexis where she was to go but each time he had picked something up Vladimir had warned him to put it down. He couldn't believe he had turned someone so childish into a vampire. He was going to regret this for the rest of his immortal life, especially since he didn't seem to want to disappear anywhere either.

Vladimir was fed up with Louie's questions; he titled his head towards his young vampire and shook it once more. "You know we cannot. We have to let Daniel's kin do his work. After the noise stops we can go down. Sit down and read a book. You are giving me a headache with your pacing" Vladimir went back to writing on the paper at his desk – he didn't know what he was doing. He was scribbling; he couldn't concentrate on anything enough to work.

Vladimir had been a great business man and had always worked from his office; he had studied many things along the business side of life and right now he wished he could dig in and forget about everything that was happening down stairs. He couldn't do that. "How can you just sit there? I thought you cared for her. I may be just fun and games but I'm pretty sure Mr. Fangy pants down there wouldn't give her the same credit" Louie hissed towards Vladimir trying to keep his voice low – he had no option in that, Vladimir had used his sire bond to order him to stay quiet, vocally at least.

That was why he kept trying to bang and make other sorts of noises. Vladimir was at a lost, sure he was at his wits end with Louie but the young vampire had a point. They didn't know about Caleb and although he was one of Daniel's kin that didn't mean he would take it easier on a girl who was a werewolf – it meant quite the opposite in fact. Vladimir opened his voice to speak but was cut off by a small cry from down stairs, they both recognised it as Alexis and both their eyes shot to the door. Vladimir had to take the high ground on this; he ground his teeth before speaking. "Leave it Louie. He knows what he's doing" Vladimir relaxed himself and sat back in his chair trying to calm his nerves by closing his eyes and tilting it back over the chair.

Louie threw his arms up in frustration, swearing a few times in French before he stormed off to the corner of room and sat on the chair "I hope chu know what you're doing" folding his arms in front of his chest, he dramatically stared towards his feet like a child would if they weren't getting what they wanted.

There was only so much Vladimir could take and never in his life did he think after becoming a vampire that he would care for someone like a father would. He cared for Louie of course but he was more like a stake in his side, and any harm that Louie brought to himself was Louie's fault. But with Alexis – it was different.

Alexis was a child when she came to him. She had appeared with Daniel, those big green eyes staring up at her, he wouldn't have been able to tell she was a werewolf unless Daniel had told him. The young girl's hair was in a mess and she needed a good wash, she had been though a lot and she stunk of smoke, the fire that killed her kind was more than likely the reason of that.

That had been when Vladimir had been entrusted with the job to raise the young werewolf as a guard dog. He had tried to keep his distance but that had not worked out like he had planned. Vladimir's eyes opened as he stared up at the ceiling

"I hope so" he whispered and then repeated it once more as he closed his eyes again. "I hope so"

7

Permission, Granted

Alexis felt her head vibrating as if someone was jumping on it. She groaned and tried to dig herself more into her bed. Her eyes were sore and she felt more tired than what she did when she had went to sleep in the first place.

Someone *was* jumping on her bed; she could feel the covers stretching with every jump, her body reacting as the bed was pushed up and then down again. *Why was this happening? What time was it?*

Whoever it was – she wanted it to stop.

It was far too much especially when she felt so tired. “Get up sleepy head. Are you going to sleep all night? I thought that was what you didn’t want to do” The strong French voice of Louie was pulled forward and it only made her groan more, pulling the covers over her head. *Why was he here? Why couldn't he just stay gone?* He didn't seem to be going away. He bounced more, trying to grab her attention singing her name in an out of tune voice trying to annoy her and wake her up.

As much as she hated him, she couldn't help but smile at his attempt to wake her up. His attempts were ruthless and she pushed the covers down to see him. "Alright. I get it. I'm up" Alexis voice was full of her smile and he couldn't help but look up towards a happy Louie who bounced down into bed beside her on top of the covers. He was annoying and comforting, he was something she was used too and had been for most of her years. "Now this seems like the perfect place for moi. I should stay here more often" Louie teased, his eyebrows wiggling as he moved his arms around Alexis in a suggestive gesture.

Alexis let out a throaty laugh and shook her head, removing his arm and slipping out of bed. The full time keeping her eyes on him, she had seen what he could do before and she wasn't about to be tricked out of it by the French vampire. "Now you're dreaming Louie. Not a chance" A laugh came from him as he snuggled down into her bed and put both of his hands behind his head, cradling it. "As amusing as the two of you are. I believe we came here for a reason, Louie" Alexis spun around at the voice to find Vladimir standing with a smile on his face watching the bickering. His arms were folded over his chest and his eyes seemed warm and inviting. She rushed forward to Vladimir and gave him a hug, her arms winding around him and her head pushed into his chest, he was taller than her and his head could rest nicely on her head.

He felt uncomfortable when she normal gave him a hug, he had never shown this type of affection to anyone as a vampire and he had never intended too. But for some reason he looked forward to his hugs from the little pup. He squeezed her back and then pushed her backwards slightly. "Where have you guys been? I looked everywhere, you just disappeared." Alexis looked towards Vladimir, her eyes staring up at him before turning to look towards Louie – who had moved to the edge of her bed, his legs dangling over the edge of it and his arms dangling in between them.

He too was staring at Vladimir not knowing what to explain to the young girl they had looked over. They had never both disappeared away from her and Louie was sure she would know something was up if he began to try and explain.

Besides Louie thought they might as well tell her the truth. After all it wasn't there idea and they hadn't agreed to it – well Louie hadn't anyway. As an older vampire, Vladimir knew that there would be more trouble if she found out the truth so instead he did the only logical thing. He lied. "We had some business to take care of and it was the perfect time since Caleb was here. You couldn't get into any trouble with him here"

Although he spun the lie he had stopped smiling and was sure he couldn't believe it fully himself. He just hoped she would. Alexis nodded her head although she didn't understand the logic behind it; she knew that neither of them would put her in danger. They must have trusted Caleb and therefore she was left with him. Although she didn't know what else to say so she left that for them to speak. Thy had obviously come here for a reason considering Vladimir's first words and it had nothing to do with their disappearance yesterday.

Otherwise he would have come out and said something without her having to ask – Alexis could tell that he felt awkward speaking about their time away and she assumed that must have meant that it hadn't went to plan.

So Alexis knew not to bring it back up again, it would do no good and scare Vladimir away to his office. Vladimir straightened himself up and paced across the room a few times before turning to face Alexis, he felt nervous about what he was going to tell her and he didn't want her to go anywhere. But this was what she wanted and for once Daniel had agreed to something the young pup wanted. Which in this case was good, Vladimir was finally able to give her something. He was finally able to do something for her. "After much …consideration. I have contacted the local school, which is only a few blocks away and they have allowed you to join at the beginning of next week. On the Monday you will take on the subjects that are available since they have just started their second term. Their school days are…long. Monday to Thursday. 7:45 till 2:10" Vladimir's voice was almost robotic although he kept his eyes on Alexis looking to see her reaction.

Fear coursed through her - that was a long time to spend away from her family and also a long time to spend with people. Innocent people. Especially people she didn't know, people that she could potentially put into danger. Alexis steeled her emotions and nodded her head, she was ready. She could do this without thinking she was going to hurt anyone. She had supressed her werewolf gene; there was no fear of it coming back.

She had researched it enough times. The books, the webpage, everything she had read said the same thing – supressing the werewolf gene is difficult but if done at a young age because of tragic reasons, then the werewolf itself can only be raised by a strong feeling of love or hate. – Alexis knew that by love it meant to find the werewolves mate, which without the werewolf gene she could not do. Both the wolf and she had to feel love in order to be completely in love which couldn't happen if she supressed said gene.

As for hatred, she believed that no one could ever push her to hate someone, not with a passion that equalled love. That was why she figured she would be safe, no matter what she did. A smile lit her lips and she couldn't help but feel tearful as she looked towards her *'father'* like figure. He had done this for her – he had gone out of his way to get her in to a normal school and sure he didn't seem happy about it but he was letting her go.

Alexis smiled before pushing herself back into Vladimir's chest, her arms were tight around him and she couldn't help but let a tear fall from her eyes in his chest. "Thank you" she whispered knowing that he would be able to hear it. He was always able to hear it. Vladimir knew this meant a lot to her that was why he was allowing this to happen. He knew that she would be able to take care of herself and if the worst happened and the vampires wanted to take her away, she needed to be able to handle herself in the outside world.

Which she wasn't going to learn being cooped up here all the time. He nodded his head not thinking any words could handle what he was feeling right now. His eyes closed and before both of them knew it, someone else had joined in on the hug.

Alexis's eyes opened and she tried to twist her head to see. Vladimir smirked, knowing exactly who it was. "I felt left out; this was such an emotional moment. I needed to interrupt before our guest felt it" Louie interrupted with his dramatic accent. Vladimir pulled out of the hug, straightening himself up; Louie however held his grip on the struggling Alexis. He pulled her up tighter. "Louie, come on let go" She struggled to get any grip on him to push him away.

A smile traced her lips before Louie burst out laughing and let her fall to the ground. She stared up at the two people who had raised her a smile evident on her face. Vladimir smiled back for a moment before composing himself. "You best get yourself ready. The headmaster gave me a list of everything that you should have read and have to be up to date. I took the pleasure of setting them out in the library. You should catch up in there for the next few days." Alexis nodded her head pleased how much Vladimir still seemed to do for her, even when she disobeyed him. Even if it wasn't intentional. Taking a big breath she stood up from the ground and began to head out of the room. "Thanks you guys. I'll get started right away" she began to move faster in order to get to the library. She had never felt so happy but yet so scared. Her emotions were so conflicting.

This was everything she had wanted. She wanted to be normal; she wanted to be able to breathe in the life. She didn't want to have a life that was werewolf like and she didn't want to have a life that was just vampires. She loved her guardian's, there was no doubt about that but the thought of a life without danger, where she could be normal seemed much more plausible if she was able to go to school.

Alexis slowed down as she hit the stairs; her eyes followed the winding path to the library before she followed them up. She had watched many movies and each one made high school seem different. There was however a few things that remained constant – the kids were all split into groups depending on their personality and no one seemed to attend all the classes. Alexis didn't want to do either. She wanted to learn as much as she could and stay away from as many people as she could. *What could be the worst thing about school?*

If Vladimir was letting her go there then nothing could be that bad. She would be ready for going to school, moving into the library she saw the pile of books and notebooks Vladimir had left out for her. The library was dark, all the furniture was dark mahogany and most of the books were reds and blacks. There was no dust in the place, it was always well kept and lovely looking.

There was a round table in the centre of the room surrounded by comfortable and supportive chairs. With a deep breath she picked up her first book and opened it, ready to start reading it. "I heard the good news. How long have you been trying to get this then?" the deep voice from the corner of the room, Alexis recognised it right away and turned around. She hadn't even realised someone else was in the room, she cursed herself under her breath. She needed to pay more attention to the world around her. She was going to do no good if she couldn't even notice things. "School?" Caleb questioned, he wasn't that much older than her. He had only been turned into a vampire for a couple of decades now and he was sure school couldn't have changed that much since he had went.

It hadn't seemed that interesting. In fact it was the complete opposite.

School had been boring for Caleb, he couldn't have waited to finish, to get away from people he called his friends and to start living his life away from both his parents and his siblings. He couldn't understand why someone would want to go to school.

Especially when they got the choice not too. Alexis's felt her cheeks blush and she pushed her hands into the lap as she lowered her head to answer the question. "I guess a part of me has always been curious about school. But I haven't actually asked to go up until yesterday. It looks interesting and I've never been out of this place. This might give me a chance to see what life is really like" She felt nervous and she wasn't sure why? She had only just met Caleb and yet when he questioned her about school it was as if they had known each other for years.

They had spent a few hours together training and ten minutes with him of his first night – out of both those meetings all she could tell from him was that he had a double personality and that he cared for her in his own way. He wanted to help her.

Which she couldn't understand. He seemed Bipolar. She titled her head up to look at him, a curious look on her face. He stared at her, the same blank expression Vladimir often used. It had to be a vampire thing. Alexis felt her eyes start to move away from him awkwardly. She never felt comfortable with someone staring at her.

There didn't seem to be any reason. "I see" Caleb mused "You want it because you have never had it. Human nature. Very surprising for a wolf"

That last word hut Alexis like a ton of bricks. That was all he thought of her, he knew she was a wolf and he was trying to train her because someone had told him too. He didn't care for her. Alexis couldn't let anything he did or said bother her. She had to tell herself that it wasn't real.

That everything he did was out of duty, not because he wanted too. Alexis stood up from her chair irrationally, words coming to her mouth without thinking. She wasn't sure what to say or what to do. "I need to study. I need to get ready for this. I don't see why it bothers you so much. Just leave. I don't need you watching me for this" Alexis felt her head pulsating and her breath hitch at the uncertainty of her voice.

He was a vampire and something about him wasn't right, so she should treat him as a threat – yet something in her body said that she couldn't, something told her that she was safe with him. She hated it. "If you wish" Caleb spoke after staring at her for a minute, he was curious of the young pup. Every time he spoke about her '*other*' side she would flinch and react badly towards it. It was a complete change of persona, something he couldn't understand.

Something he wanted to understand as well. After a few more minutes he moved out of the room and towards the left, his room wasn't that far away from the library. He could listen and watch over her from the room he was given, he didn't turn back he merely paced his way to his room. Alexis felt torn, he just left but she couldn't complain. She had been the one to tell him to leave.

Alexis fell to her seat rubbing her face to try and rub the emotion away. Her head felt like a black hole everything getting dragged into the middle and eventually she would disappear completely. She needed to focus on something else; her hand touched the books as she pulled it on to the table. She had the exact thing to distract her right here and she was going to use it. She was going to study. She was going to get ready and enjoy school.

No one could take that away from her. No matter what.

8

Time to be cold

Over the next few days, Alexis spent most of her time in the Library or on the computer researching what she needed within school, making sure she was prepared for her start on Monday. She needed bags, books– each class was supplied with a different Utensil that was needed. She needed to feel ready.

Which she didn't feel she would be.

Vladimir helped her study as much as he could before retiring to his room and disappearing on Friday night like he often did; Alexis had grown up used too his Friday disappearances; she had often guessed what he was doing, feeding from humans – a secret lover, a debt he had to pay, check in with Daniel, feeding.

Louie tried to offer her help but mostly he just annoyed her with his comments on how humans behaved and how much he was going to miss her around the place.

The French vampire always seemed to be over dramatic. Alexis often wondered if he was bored and if he would really miss her because he wouldn't have anyone to talk to around the house anymore. Caleb and Alexis trained every second day for two hours.

Caleb acted different with her, he taught her the exact same and made sure she could easily defend herself as well as attack her opponents – the part that different was the fun, joking Caleb seemed to be few and far between. He used to be able to let go. She started to look for those times.

When he would eventually just let go. The Sunday before her day of school was her day of fighting with Caleb, it gave her a break from her studying although she didn't want too. "You realise that sitting in with those books all day is going to make you lose your mind" Caleb commented as he stood against the door in the Library. Alexis turned towards him, she was tired, her eyes were red and there were bags under her eyes.

A laugh echoed on her throat that seemed dry, she needed a drink. She kept trying to remember the basic needs for herself but lately with all the worry of school, she had forgotten.

When had she last taken a drink? When had she last been to the toilet? Slept? "I've not been in here for that long" Alexis countered, a small smile tried to pull on her face. "You've been here for 9 hours straight" That was something Alexis wasn't expecting to hear, she was really in there for that long?

"Oh…" She found herself trying to rethink where her time had gone. *What time was it now? Had she skipped past a day? It was now Sunday?* She dug into her pocket for the '*new'* phone Vladimir had bought her for going to school.

Programmed with Vladimir's and Louie's number in it for emergency circumstances. The phone stated it was Sunday and that it was 7 o'clock in the morning. She let out a groan and pushed her head down on to the table. "I must have lost track of time." Caleb couldn't help but smile and move in to lift her chin up to look at him. He was being caring again; it was always a switch with him. He could be so lovely and kind one moment and then the next he was rough and stern. “It’s alright. Are you strong enough to learn something or would you prefer to have a lesson after you sleep?” he questioned with general intrigue. He hadn’t lived with a human in two decades and even though it was so short of time he forgot how much some people needed to sleep and Alexis seemed to be different from everyone else. She would sleep half of the night and half of the day, which meant she was up half of the night with the vampires and the vampires were ‘*technically*’ up the second half for her.

That was all going to need to change now. She was going to need to get into a ‘*human*’ routine. Sleeping at night and up all day, Caleb wondered how she would cope; she had been in a vampire’s timetable for a long time.

Vladimir had been trying to get her into that schedule lately but with this last night it seemed knocked out of touch. She shook her head and stood up out of Caleb’s clasp. “I’m fine to learn for a couple of hours. Vladimir said I have to get used to staying up all day and sleeping all night. I guessed I messed up that last night but I have to keep myself up today otherwise school will be more difficult tomorrow" Alexis rubbed her eyes, now that she was back to normality instead of in one of her books she seemed to be more tired. She tried to stop herself from yawning but finally let herself be over taken by one.

Caleb chuckled slightly, before keeping the amused look on his face. "If you have a couple of hours now and then stay up till 9 you should be able to get a good night's sleep and be ready for your high school in the morning. I assure you" Alexis stared towards Caleb, sometimes she wanted to question him, she wanted to understand why he could be so cold to her sometimes and yet in moments like this –he could be so kind, so caring.

It was giving her whiplash, but instead of asking or saying anything she merely nodded her head. It seemed right. "Will you wake me up in a couple of hours then?" Alexis asked after a moment, her blue eyes staring up at the brunette eyed vampire. "I will" Caleb answered before pulling her towards him, he moved out of the way so that she would glide past him towards the door, urging her to get some more rest.

"Now go and sleep" Alexis yawned at the same time she nodded her head, she didn't look back knowing she was tired. She began to head down the stairs towards her bedroom to get some sleep.

Caleb let her sleep; he stood at her door as soon as he knew she was sleeping. He was curious; he had never seen someone so excited about something. She had stayed awake all night just to study for school. This was someone that he would have laughed at, that people would bully.

Surely he had to do something to help her, to warn her. His head tilted to the side, but she could look after herself. She wasn't some human that he had to protect. She was a werewolf. She was also able to defend herself, he had been training her and he could feel the strength running through her arms. He knew she was able to protect herself. He shouldn't worry about her.

He shouldn't worry about her for many reasons and her being bullied was the least of these.

Daniel was going to kill him if he didn't make her turn into a werewolf, he was supposed to be working on her rage – trying to push her to her limits but instead he was standing at her door thinking of ways to protect her? Now that didn't seem right.

He didn't seem to be in the right state of mind. He stiffened himself up and marched over to her bed, he paused looking at her sleeping. She was so delicate, so gentle and so peaceful. He didn't want to disturb her, yet he had promised her.

Also if she didn't get up, she wouldn't be able to sleep tonight. Caleb had let her sleep long enough, she had gone to bed at seven and now it was eleven. She needed to get up and eat lunch as well as train. He took a big breath and nudged her, she groaned slightly. "Alexis" Caleb spoke sternly and Alexis pulled up the covers a little more.

A shake of Caleb's head had him almost smiling; he steeled himself against that thought and grabbed the covers at the edge of her bed. *She wanted woken up* Caleb thought before pulling the covers with all his power towards him and on the floor in front of him. Alexis spun in the bed; she had grabbed on to the covers and she regretted that fact. Her eyes sprung open and she managed to let go of the covers just before she went off the bed with them. Her direction had changed on the bed and she now lay vertically on the bed, her hair pulled over her face and her chin bounced off the mattress.

"Right. Time for training" Caleb's voice spoke and she lifted her head to greet it, she couldn't see through the tangles of hair covering her face. Caleb had moved towards the door only looking back to see if she was following him. "Hurry up" He added on before leaving her door and heading towards the gym.

Alexis was stunned for a moment before she stumbled off of her bed and headed towards her bathroom to strip and get ready for training. *What time was it? How long had she been sleeping?* Alexis felt so disorientated; she rubbed her eyes and got into a shower, hoping that it would wake her up. She moved as quickly as she could and got washed and then shortly after got dressed. Pulling on her shoes she stumbled out her bedroom door to head towards the gym. She rushed along trying to catch a glimpse at the clocks around the house to see if she could see the time but no matter how hard she tried the clocks were always just out of her view.

Towards the last few doors she gave up and rushed to the gym. Caleb had pulled himself down to a tank top and shorts, her towel was over his shoulder and he had moved mats into the middle of the room.

Stunned for a moment she moved to the middle of the room, stopping before the mats. "Ready Chief" Alexis pulled on one of her big smiles hoping that it would come across well. Caleb looked up at her, his face held an un-amused expression, his eyes held a caring perspective in them; if she hadn't seen it before she would have missed it for sure. Shaking her head she tried to avoid what was happening, she decided she wasn't going to get caught up in his emotional turmoil. Alexis decided she was going to focus on her workout and defensive training, especially since she was scared about tomorrow.

What happened if she ran into bullies or werewolves? She needed to know how to defend herself and the only person that seemed to be helping her was Caleb. He had taught her more in the past two weeks that Louie had in the last year. "So...What are we learning today?" Alexis tried to make conversation with him, more light-hearted tones always made him easier to be around. It normally made him friendly as well but she didn't think that was going to happen this time. Caleb lifted himself from the ground after he placed the last mat in place and rubbed his hands against his shorts; he grabbed the towel from his shoulders and flung it to the side of the room. "We'll just go over everything we've learned before to make sure you remember it all" Caleb looked her over waiting for her to object before he moved forward, shaking out his limbs so he was ready to fight.

Alexis began to stretch out just like Caleb had taught her too, making her legs heat up she bent them behind her and started to jog on the spot, she moved her head to the side a few times and shook out her hands.

Caleb began from the beginning going over everything he had taught her and Alexis remembered everything. Not only because he had been a good teacher on these things but because she had wanted to learn.

Which made a big difference, she knew this from when Vladimir had taught her the different subjects growing up. With English and other Language subjects she had always wanted to learn them and that had shown in her work, but with Maths it had been lacking. She had found it a boring subject and that had also shown in the outcome of her work. She didn't understand the value of numbers and she never knew why they were so important, sure she loved words and she loved how words and numbers could blend together to make a story but Algebra just killed her – if she could avoid that subject then she would.

Constantly. After a couple of hours of practice, Caleb stopped –he hadn't broken a sweat like he normally did. Alexis felt warm and she knew sweat would be dripping down her forehead but she wasn't ready to stop training yet. She wanted to tire herself out.

Taking in deep breaths, she tried to calm her breathing down. She was panting almost, her heartbeat going faster than it normally went. "May I ask you a question?" Caleb found himself questioning the young wolf without actually thinking, he had thought about this question many times but he had always refused to ask it. He didn't really think it was important and he couldn't justify asking that question.

Now he didn't care, he wanted to ask the question and he didn't care if there was no justifying it – it was time he knew. Alexis looked at him trying to assess what he was going to ask her, if the question was going to be one she could answer. But from his eyes she couldn't tell anything so instead of saying anything she bounced her head into a small nod waiting for him to ask. "Why do you want to learn how to defend yourself and fight?" his eyes questioned with someone she hadn't notice before.

Sadness. Caring?

Alexis head tilted to the side, she felt like her insides should panic, her heart rate should have increased and the sweat of being nervous should have been dripping down her. But instead she was ready for it; she had tried avoiding this question since she had asked to be trained. With Vladimir and Louie she had joked it off saying she needed to be able to protect herself from Louie's advances or anyone else like him.

Now with Caleb she felt like she wanted to tell him the truth, she felt like he was someone that would understand why she felt the way she did. Alexis didn't need to justify anything to anyone but still to Caleb she felt like she owed him something. He had come into her home and apart from acting like a smart aleck, egotistic vampire – he had treated her with respect and taught her not only how to fight but how to have fun with someone her age. He hadn't just been training her, he would play games with her, hide and seek was something that was easily played in such a big house.

He had woke her up in the middle of the night not long after she had went to sleep to watch the stars fly across the sky as he told her to make a wish.

The bond she had created with Caleb was one both of them seemed to ignore when it came down to it, one minute they would be so close you would think they were more than friends and then the next they were cold towards each other and acted as if they were natural enemies. That was how it seemed to be. None of them confronted what was right in front of them and it was like they were each waiting for the other to make the move. But the two of them wouldn't make that move, both refused.

A shrug followed Caleb's words before Alexis spoke. "I know we're not always going to be stuck in this house and I did want to get out of this place sooner or later so I thought I needed a way to defend myself. School was my best option because it's sort of an in between so I don't have to completely leave the house by myself, it's just half the day. Vladimir has told me about the werewolves, and how dangerous they can be to humans never mind each other and I'd hate to run into one of them and not know how to defend myself against them. I know he said the best thing to do is run but I bet you sometimes you don't get the chance to run. You only get the chance to fight. I guess I just want to be ready for anything. No matter what the danger. Plus I bet not all vampires are as nice as you guys" Alexis was staring down at her feet by the send of her speech. She felt nervous and she had tried to get through her reason very quickly wondering what Caleb would think of her when he knew the truth, she half wondered if he would laugh at her because of it. She hoped not.

The room was silent.

Nothing was said and her words hung in the air like a bad smell. She dragged her eyes up from the ground to look at Caleb and again he looked at her with his caring eyes, he smiled slightly. "I understand, you don't need to explain to me how you feel but I do understand and I am glad I could teach you" She had expected anything apart from that, she held her surprise back and smiled towards him. He could be so kind sometimes that she didn't expect it especially in times when he had been acting so cold.

"Now go and get something to eat so you're ready for school tomorrow and pack your bag. You're better getting everything ready tonight for school. Vladimir is looking for you anyway you better go and see him" Alexis smiled towards him nodding her head before hugging him "Thank you" Caleb tensed and he couldn't bring himself to hug her back, she had never shown this much affection for him before, he hadn't been shown this affection from anyone before not even in his family when he was human.

A smile curved his lips as he pulled her off of him and turned her around to the door pushing her out the door. She looked nervously up towards him, wondering how he had reacted to her hug. But he didn't seem overly effective towards it. "Good Luck" She was pushed towards the door, her steps making an echo against the ground as she moved to find Vladimir.

9

Je te dis merdel

The room was pitch black, there was something different about it though. She couldn't see around her, she couldn't see any walls. The room seemed to be never ending. Where was she? How was she here? She was trapped. Her arms were strapped to the chair, her eyes were pushed tight shut. Her hair draped across her face, it stuck to her like glue.

The sweat was running down her; her breathing began to pick up, faster and faster. She was too scared to open her eyes to assess her surroundings. She could hear her heart beating loudly in her ears and her chest hurt. She tried to move her hands and the ropes rubbed against her wrists causing them to go red. Her teeth grinded together as she resisted the urge to call out although she couldn't remember the reason for not calling out.

This wasn't right, she felt like something wasn't right. Her legs tried to kick out and didn't get very far; they were pulled against the leg of the chair.

The air was cool, yet she was sweating? How did that work? She couldn't understand it. She cursed under her breath trying to fight against the pain and trying to get her arms out of the ropes or her legs. She focused her breathing, deep breaths in and out, in and out. She had to get her breathing back to normal before she went into a full blown panic attack.

A low growl came from behind her and her breath hitched. She turned her head slightly not wanting to look behind her but wanting to hear how close it was. The growl seemed to be all around her, she couldn't work out how close it was or how far away it was.

The growl began to get louder and she could feel the shaking start in her legs and move up through her body. She could feel a hot breath against her neck. She turned her head to the front and her eyes shot open. She refused to look at it; she refused to acknowledge what was behind her. She shook her head. "This is not real....This is not real" She started repeating over and over again under her breath.

A chuckle came from behind her; it ruffled through the beast as if it was laughing at her, as if it heard exactly what she said. As if it understood what she was saying. She could hear its paws against the ground and she waited to feel the teeth against her neck but instead she felt something warm and wet.

*A tongue. It rolled around the back of her neck and she shivered in reaction. She heard another growl and then....*shot up in her bed.

The sweat was dripping from her. Her covers had moved off the bed and her hair stuck in different positions all over her head. She felt disorientated. She was lost. Her eyes adjusted to the room she was in and she recognised it as her own. She was in her own bedroom. She turned to the side; her clock was by her bed.

It was 6:31 am in the morning. She lay back down trying to catch her breath. It was only a nightmare. She had had that nightmare before but it hadn't been the same nightmare. It was different. There had been one difference. Normally she woke up with the animal biting her neck, but this time it had licked her. It had run its tongue along her neck. *Why had it done that?* She was confused. She needed to shake that off.

Today was a busy day, why had she had that dream that night? It should have been any other night. This was important. She was going to school. She tried to forget about the terrible dream she had just endured and got up from her bed to get ready for school.

Within moments she had Vladimir and Louie in helping her get ready, making sure she had everything she needed. She floated by, her excitement was increasing, and her dream was long forgotten just like every other one she had. Caleb had briefly spoken to her, wishing her good luck. But that was all she had heard from him and he had retired away. Alexis didn't notice, she was ushered towards the door and told exactly where she was going.

Although she wasn't walking. They had hired a car to take her; Vladimir explained to her that this was going to be her driver. He was going to take her to school and pick her up every day. Which was new to her, as soon as she started to fight against his words, he hushed her. It had to be part of the agreement of her being allowed to attend school.

It was a small price to pay but it was something she could live with, she hugged both Vladimir and Louie and slipped into the car. Millions of thoughts were streaming through her head and she couldn't properly think what this place was going to be like. She had never even seen a school before, without it being some sort of fiction. She could imagine of course and picture things she had seen in movies or television shows.

But were they real? Was that what it was really like? She shook her head and started to look out the window. "First time in school" the driver spoke to her, surprised she stared on at him for a minute. She hadn't expected someone Vladimir had hired to take her to school to actually talk to her. He had hired many people- humans- over the years, maids, cooks, she had lost count of the numbers but every time she tried to speak to them it was as if they were mute. She smiled slightly, this could only be good for her "Yes" she spoke quietly and he looked back in the mirror, she could see his eyes watching her, with a smile. He was nice. He was slightly older than Vladimir looked mid 40's. His grey hair was short and topped with a small hat, his eyes were deep brown. He had a warm brown coat on; she couldn't see anything else because of the way the car was positioned.

"Nervous huh?" The driver had a deep voice, it was rough as if he had been smoking a lot, and he had a deep cough that often followed his words. He seemed to always be catching for some air. "A little bit" Alexis was brought up to speak to everyone and to act properly no matter who that person was even if they were rude to her.

Vladimir had taught her that in 3 different languages and he had made sure that the way she spoke was always proper without any lucid qualities. Alexis of course hadn't known any different. Louie spoke foully at first, but Vladimir had often spoken about that being his upbringing and how he had been dragged up rather than brought up. She didn't know whether he had been joking or not. Vladimir had a way of making everything seem real and important and that was a quality she admired in him so much.

She knew it could be a very dangerous quality but as far as she could tell he had never used it against her or anyone in that way. She didn't think a child was supposed to feel proud of their guardians but she felt very proud to have Vladimir as hers. She could have ended up with a lot worse, she knew that not all vampires were nice and not all would have given her the privileges that Vladimir and Louie had. She was happy that she had gotten to live with them. It was fate. "Don't be nervous. It's not all that bad. You never know you might enjoy it. I'll tell you, I remember goin to school as if it were yesterday. It was good. You learned things, you got to make thing. I am sure you will love it." The older gentleman spoke kindly in the front;

Alexis pulled a smile to her face. She wasn't worried about anything he had just said.

School was something she knew she would enjoy, she loved to read, she loved to learn and she had been brought up to know that every new thing you learned was important.

What she was nervous about were the pupils, the other children. She couldn't remember the last time she had met someone her age. Someone who was actually her age and didn't just look it. The people she was normally around had lived for more than 40 years at the very least, even if they looked close to her age.

But how could she explain that to a complete stranger? How could she explain that to anyone? She couldn't. The world of vampires and werewolves were supposed to be hidden. No one was supposed to know about them. If she started speaking like that, she would be accused of living in a fantasy land and that would be the very minimum that would happen.

They would more than likely lock her up, that couldn't ever happen. *What if they found out she was a werewolf?* Then things would really start to kick off.

A shake of her head and she forced that little voice deep down inside of her. She wasn't going to bring anything like that up right now. She wasn't going to think of the worst situations like she normally did. She was going to think more positively; like whom she was going to meet on the first day, what classes she was going to be taking.

Those seemed like a better thing to be thinking about. She sunk back into the back seat of the car. "Thank you" She whispered towards the man before he was turning on to the street with the school. Alexis had been counting exactly where she was going, following the directions that Vladimir had given her. She took in a deep breath and sat straight up, admiring the school from the window.

The place was nothing like she had expected but yet it felt that much better. Her eyes lit up with the site of it. It was a small building, maybe two stories but it was long. The windows were long as well and the top of the school stretched into a point. The middle of the school instead of a square window had a round one.

Both sides of the school were symmetrical. Alexis could tell that just by looking. There were two entrances either side but also big doors right under the round window. The building was rough casted brick, it was mostly cream but there had been some damaged by children's spray paint drawings.

The bits like that were colourful in complete comparison to the cream but still Alexis found it amazing. "That's us here" The man had stopped the car near the front entrance, the gates were black but anybody could see they had worn down over time, with students climbing over them and age attacking them there was no wonder.

The man turned around to face Alexis, he had a smile on his face and Alexis could see that he was missing a couple of teeth. He had a moustache on his face that was also grey matching his hair. "You'll be fine Kiddo. Go on beat it" A joking smile pinched his cheeks as he waved her away from the car.

Alexis was quick to grab her back and move out of it, she turned to wave as he drove away before turning back to the school. *Was she ready for this?* She didn't think so, but she moved forward knowing that she needed to attempt this anyway.

10

Welcome to hell school

"I think that is us then. We have spaces in English 12, American Government, Foreign Language Honours and College Prep" The teacher tilted her head to the side, her glasses pushed to the end of her nose.

The wrinkles covered her face making her look older than she probably was. Her eyes had left a vibrant brown colour and had moved more towards a dull hazel. Her body was pressed against the table and her green coloured clothes didn't compliment her at all. She pursed her lips together peering down at the schedule she had drawn up for Alexis before looking up to examine the student in front of her. "Would that be too your liking?" She asked although by the tone of her voice, Alexis nodded her head not wanting to disagree.

Vladimir had obviously tried to get her the best subjects possible with what was available, which couldn't have been much considering they were already through their first term and people would be just beginning to settle in to their subjects.

Alexis didn't bother with what subjects she had been giving she would be able to work through anything, she had learned enough with tutors, Vladimir and herself. She knew how to do the most complicated equation with any working that was needed.

Vladimir had made sure of that but she couldn't hate him for wanting to teach her.

She would be very thankful that she wasn't going in to school unprepared. "Very well. Your Classes are under each subject which will help you find each class. Every third period you shall report to your Home room Classroom. That's your third class which is straight down the hall and the second last Classroom on your left. Your first class is up the stairs, room L41, half way along the corridor don't forget to knock before you enter"

The older women handed Alexis the timetable in her hand before pointing out the door and towards the end of the corridor. Alexis's eyes couldn't help but follow the old women's out stretched fingers before returning to her face.

"Thank you Ms" Alexis smiled although the women didn't return it; she merely turned back to her computer and got on with her work. Alexis left without being effected by the older women, through the doors and started her way down the corridor. Her eyes drifted over her timetable. Alexis had never been to school, she had never followed a timetable, she half wondered if she was going to be able to do such a thing. Her eyes widened and she looked at it.

She was going to be busy. It was a packed schedule. But she couldn't help but look forward to it.

There was so much to look forward too. English was one that although was very simple it was the one she most looked forward to. In fact she thought that the timetable was rather short compared to some of the movies she had watched and the books she had read. Normally they went to school till Friday.

	Monday	Tuesday	Wednesday	Thursday
7.45 – 8:30	English 12 L41	College Prep G4	College Prep G4	American Government 1 H52
8:35 – 9:20	English 12 L41	"Free"	American Government 1 H52	American Government 1 H52
9:25 – 9:40	Home Room			
9:45 – 10:30	Foreign Language Honours G16	American Government 1 H52	Foreign Language Honours G16	"Free"
10:35 – 11:20	Foreign Language Honours G16	English 12 L41	Foreign Language Honours G16	Foreign Language Honours G16
11:20 – 12:30	Lunch			
12:35 – 1:20	American Government 1 H52	Foreign Language Honours G16	College Prep G4	English 12 L41
1:25 – 2:10	College Prep G4	Foreign Language Honours G16	College Prep G4	English 12 L41

Not that she was complaining.

She was happy just to be able to attend school. A smile moved across her face. She needed to give Vladimir another hug when she saw him next.

He always seemed to know what to do to make her happy. He was the father that she wished she had and he was more of a guardian to her than anyone else had ever been. She didn't know what she would do without him. Not that she ever wanted to be without him.

How did this even happen? How had he managed to get the Elder to agree to such a request?

She looked up when she hit the end of the corridor to find stairs that lead up to the top of the school, according to the older women in the office. Alexis didn't doubt that the woman wasn't the headmistress or anything along those lines but she knew she was telling her the truth. Her eyes drifted around the school at the lockers that lined the walls between the doors of Classrooms.

Every class seemed to already be in motion, she took a deep breath. She was a new pupil, that couldn't be that bad. She pushed open the door to the stairs and walked through, her eyes looking towards her feet she counted the steps up the stairs, glancing at everything as she passed it. The school had recently been done up - everything seemed clean and unscratched, there was no pictures up and nothing to signify this was a school in any way.

There were dark curtains draping the long window on the stairs, although pulled open to let the light come in. Alexis half turned to look out the window as she passed by, still walking she didn't want to be any later for the class than she was already.

Outside was a forest of chimneys and houses, Alexis had never seen such a view. She paused for a moment, her timetable in hand and her eyes casting over the scenery in front of her, she was breathless. She could see green in between the houses as well as far in the distance. The trees in the distance looked like toys; they were so small, she could hardly make out where one tree ended and another began.

No human could have made out the different tree's, another reason she knew she was different – Her eye sight. She sighed and was bumped out of the road by someone. His shoulder bashed against hers causing her some pain, her hand reached up to cradle it as she moved herself back out of the road. Her eyes shooting up to look at who had bumped past her, his eyes were almost black; she could hardly catch where his pupils were. His short light brown hair was messed up and strayed to the side, he looked dangerous, everything in her told her to stand her ground, yet her mind screamed at her to run. She was stuck in position, her feet refusing to move and obey what she wanted to do.

Her eyes couldn't move from his face, he too had frozen; his eyes looked over her with scrutiny. He was assessing her, *why?* Alexis could feel the hairs on the back of her neck raising and her heart beginning to beat faster in fear. *Why wouldn't her body cooperate with her?* The boy sniffed the air and growled…he growled? Alexis's heart sunk in fear with this, what she had been afraid of all her life. *She didn't even get to have her first day in peace?* Part of her wished she hadn't even tried to come to school. It would have been much easier, it would have been safer. Vladimir was going to kill her if she got hurt, she would never be allowed out the house again.

Alexis could feel herself begin to panic; she needed to slow herself down. She knew how to protect herself. Caleb had been spending these past few weeks training her constantly. She couldn't waste it; she didn't want to waste it. She slowed her breathing down, taking a big breath in and out continuously. She wasn't going to be intimidated by another wolf. She could show she wasn't scared. That would have been good if the fear wasn't oozing out of her in those moments. She tried to put mind over matter, her mind raced with thoughts and she tried to focus them away from the negative ones and focus on those telling her she was going to be fine. He couldn't kill her in a local school, there was camera's…surely.

There were too many people.

The boy stared at her as she tackled her emotional turmoil, he seemed angry for some reason, his eyes turned towards the door she had not long come through and then back to her. He shook his head and continued down the stairs. Alexis took in a deep breath as he left through the doors, her body relaxed and her knees began to wobble. She felt like they were about to give way. Her eyes closed for a moment as she leaned on the wall; she needed to gain her focus back, she needed to get her strength back.

When she opened her eyes she knew she had to continue on whether or not he was still in this school. She couldn't let Vladimir or Louie know – they would never let her come back to school, they wouldn't even let her try another school.

This was her only shot – she could combat her fear of one werewolf. It was a big school; she might not see him again. As long as she stayed with people, or even in groups he couldn't do her any harm. She had to make friends, as soon as possible. She had to meet people that could protect her from her own species.

That was it. She had decided, she took in another big breath and tested her legs, then once she knew they were stable enough she continued up the stairs and along to her classroom. Just like the older women at the main office said she knocked on the door.

"Enter" Alexis heard a voice coming from the classroom, she felt the nerves running through her in these moments but she knew if she held out any longer she wouldn't be able to do it. She wouldn't be able to go through the door, her hand gripped the handle and she pushed on the door.

Every eye was on her and she walked into the class room and headed towards the teacher, her eyes lit up with recognition. "Ah, you must be Alexis Smith, correct?" Alexis couldn't find the words to speak, not only because she had just had a run in with a werewolf but also because she was in a room of strangers who were staring at her. She nodded her head as the teacher stood up to face the class.

A smile lit her lips and her blonde hair bounced down her back in long curls. She was beautiful, unlike anyone she had ever seen before. Her blue eyes looked on with a friendly attitude. "Students. We have a new pupil joining us today. Now I know none of you are shy since you all passed last year's talking exercise extraordinary. So let's give Alexis a warm welcome." She used hand movements to indicate towards Alexis and she turned to face the class.

The class laughed when she spoke about their talking exercise. There were around 15 pupils in the class, each one different. She couldn't focus on just one. "Let's see your time table dear and I can find someone that can help you with your classes" The teacher looked on at Alexis with her hand out stretched and Alexis handed her the piece of paper she had been gripping in her hand. It was a mess now after how tightly she had held on to it.

The blonde women stretched the timetable out and looked over it before turning towards the class. "Right does anyone have all or most of these classes? Foreign Language Honours, American Government I, English 12 and College prep" She remembered each of them and pronounced each out with a Texan accent.

Everybody was silent for a minute before someone lifted their hand up. "I have most of those classes and I know someone who takes the Language thing" The girl had red shoulder length hair that was pulled back into messy bun. Her eyes were a deep brown and she looked bored, her head rested on her hand against the table and she looked towards the teacher without even glancing at Alexis. Alexis's didn't have very high hopes for this person, especially if she wouldn't look at her or maybe that was just something humans did. Alexis wasn't sure anymore.

After all she had spent most of her times with vampires. They had a much older respect for people and that was why they looked you in the eye when they talked, they also loved to grab your full attention. Whereas humans weren't the same type of people. Especially these humans who were into their teenage years, Vladimir spoke of how arrogant some of them were. '*Youth is wasted on the young'* he had once said.

The teacher smiled with happiness and Alexis could feel how genuine she was. "Thank you, Cassie. There you go Alexis; Cassie will look after you for the day. She's a nice girl and I am sure she can answer any question that you can ask but if she can't feel free to come ask me anything" Miss Michaels answered as she handed back the girl's timetable. She ushered her to the back of classroom beside Cassie.

Still silent, Alexis moved her way through the classroom and sat herself down in the spare seat beside Cassie. Her eyes drifted towards the girl for a moment and she received a small smile. This didn't seem to be so bad. Alexis's mood perked up and she couldn't help but get on with the class. Which was more interesting than she had ever expected it to be.

Things could only look up from here she was sure. They had too. She had no other options.

11

Lion's mane

Cassie was friendly and Alexis couldn't help but feel guilty about her earlier thought. The girl had lovely red hair like a lion's mane. Cassie had let her hair out of the bun into the second period of English 12 and now Alexis couldn't help but watch it from time to time. It looked like fire stretching from her head and curling around her cheeks.

The brown eyed girl had seemed to come more alive as they went on through the class and the discussions were phenomena especially as they walked to their next class. "So where have you come from anyway? I can't tell from your accent. You don't sound like you know anything about school. You must have been in a school that was nowhere near America since I'm pretty sure all the schools are the same here" Cassie was bright, alive and radiant as they walked between classes.

Alexis wore her bag like a back pack yet Cassie had one over her left arm and it hung their like a handbag rather than a school bag.

The blue eyed girl couldn't help but smile back; she was enjoying meeting someone new, someone human for once. They didn't seem all that bad. "I have never been to school before. I was …home schooled" Of course they had stories made up about what Alexis's life was like before she attended school, Vladimir had said she would need to plan everything threw and stick to the same story. He had mentioned how nosey humans were especially with people they didn't know.

So together Alexis and Vladimir had come up with a story that was almost towards the truth. She had travelled a lot and she had been home schooled because of it. "Wow. I can't say I have ever known anyone that has been home schooled before. Which means you missed out on Home Room and end of term parties?"

Cassie was curious just like the elder vampire had said and that couldn't help but make her chuckle and shake her head in answer to the human girl's question.

"I can't say that I have. What is home room?" Alexis pronounced it out like it was a foreign word, not knowing at all what it could even mean.

Home was somewhere you lived and room was a place inside that. Considering Alexis didn't live here she had given up guessing what this class was and let it be a surprise. That was why she wanted to come to high school after all – she wanted it to be different, she wanted it to be a surprise. The red haired girl laughed out loud which was ended on a snort which Alexis smiled at – the strangeness of humans was something that Alexis enjoyed. "Home room is a class to check we are all here. It's like a registration and a guidance class all rolled up in one. It's not as strict as other classes although you do have to attend it. You can eat and drink and chat in the class which you can't normally do unless the teacher lets you. The teacher is only there to help with any problems. We can find Marie in that class

– she has your Language thing, she loves to learn all those different accents and words so you'll get on with her just fine." Cassie was talking constantly and it didn't seem like she was taking a breath. The girl acted as if she wanted to know everything and anything that came to her mind in that moment. Alexis had never quiet met anyone like her, it was most refreshing. She couldn't help but wonder if all the girls in this school acted like this, if all human girls acted like this.

There was only one way she was going to find out and that was through talking to the other girls in this school. She hadn't even been half way through the day yet.

It was time to meet more people. Cassie stopped next to a classroom and waved her hand dramatically towards it. "Here we are. Home room. I'm sure you'll be added to the register but just in case we better let Mrs. Lowlor know you are here and then we can get Marie" Cassie smiled at Alexis with a bright smile before turning into the room and heading over to the desk, Alexis fell behind her nervously. She started to fidget with the edge of her jumper.

Cassie still as cheerful as ever skipped forward until they got to the desk, she put her arms around Alexis and pulled her forward. “Miss Lowlor, here’s the new student just in case she hasn’t been added to your register yet” The teacher was short and stubby, she looked up at the girls from behind her small classes, her eyes were beady and she tilted her lip at one side. “Yes I had heard we had someone new joining our class. Miss Alexis Smith I presume?” Alexis nodded her head to the teachers question, she marked something down on her sheet and Cassie moved to pull her away from the desk. “She won’t need you anymore, just marking you as here and now we can go see Marie and I can introduce you to the rest of my friends. You will sit with us at lunch won’t you? What am I saying of course you will. You don’t know how the lunch system works but I will make sure to help you” The red haired girl went on talking and Alexis tried to keep up with everything she was saying.

A lunch system? There was a certain way you had to eat lunch? This was something that was definitely going to be confusing. She was going to have to stick to Cassie like glue especially if she was going to have to work out how to eat lunch.

Alexis was stunned momentarily, luckily Cassie noticed her look and grabbed her hand in her own. “Don’t look so worried. School isn’t that hard it’s a piece of cake you will get used to it in no time at all” The girl chimed in as she lead her down between the tables.

People were sprawled out all over the classroom – everyone was in groups – some were sitting on the tables, others were merely lying against them. They were all in heated talks about something or other, although Cassie didn’t falter in step, never once. She spoke to people as she walked through, a quick hi to certain ones she knew before she was stopping at a group of people pulling Alexis in beside her like a rag doll. She offered her a small smile before waving her arms to make sure the attention of her ‘friends’ was all on her. “Guys this is Alexis. She just joined here. Alexis this is Katie, Mary, Chris, Jack and Ashley” Alexis wasn’t sure how to great anyone in these moments, frozen in position she raised her hand to wave adding a small “Hi” in as she looked around them.

There was no Marie in there; Alexis had listened out for that name knowing that she was going to be joining a class with her in it. “Let me guess you were stuffed with Miss Popularity up here by force of behead-ment?” Chris grinned towards Alexis before turning his question towards Cassie who reacted by punching him against his shoulder. Her eyes lit up in amusement and his reacted almost like hers, his pupils dilated in enjoyment as if he had been encouraging exactly that reaction, he pulled her against him so that her back was against his chest and she burst into a fit of giggles as his hands tickled her sides. “Dear god Cassandra. Christopher you’re scaring the poor girl” Ashley stood up pulling Alexis out of the way of the two hooligans although she held the same playful grin that the other two did. “Relax Ash. You’re always so up-tight.” Cassie slipped away from Chris to join her new friend once again.

“So where have you come from Al-ex-is?” The other boy, Jack spoke from where he sat at the table, his hands placed on the desk as if holding himself there. Alexis opened her mouth to answer but before she got the chance to, Cassie spoke for her. “She’s been home schooled, for like forever. This is her first time in school. She only stays a couple of blocks from the school” She acted casually and Alexis decided to let Cassie take over answering questions for her while she could.

After all she had just repeated this very same story to her not moments ago. Cassie had milked her for enough information so that she could look like she knew Alexis more than she did. Alexis didn’t mind of course, she was happy to let Cassie answer any and all questions that were directed at her. “I don’t know how you survived without it. I don’t think anyone likes school but at the same time I don’t know how anyone could learn at home. I can hardly do homework at home” A laugh rang out from Katie’s mouth and Alexis smiled in response.

Humans were different here, different from what she expected but one thing she had expected was for them to be undisciplined and right now with Katie’s words that seemed to ring true. “Please. She speaks four different languages and is doing basically all higher and advanced higher subjects this year. She definitely doesn't have a problem learning at home" Cassie answered as she looked at her nails checking if any of them were damaged, she seemed to be acting less interested in the subject at hand although more than happy to soak up all the attention it was giving her.

A shiver ran up Alexis's spine for some unknown reason and Alexis glanced away from the group for a moment sensing that someone had to be watching her.

At first glance she couldn't see anyone, they all looked busy with in themselves and no one seemed to stand out to her in particular, so she tried to return to the conversation at hand. "Please tell me you've been shopping before, not shopping like for clothes but for like a party without parental help" Ashley looked shocked at the things that Alexis hadn't done, they had obviously been asking Cassie about what things Alexis knew about schools.

The Brunette girl smiled towards this group and leaned against the table she could feel almost touching her legs. "I have been shopping before but not with friends. I haven't had very many friends, travelling around a lot, hasn't left many options for that" Alexis shrugged her shoulders as if it didn't bother her one bit but two of the girls seemed shocked by that. They acted as if it was a sin to not have done some of these things before. "Relax Katie, Ashley. We can take her out sometime and show her what she's missing. We have parties coming up and she probably doesn't have anything to wear to them. We can help pick the right dress for each occasion, because each needs something different" Alexis had thousands of clothes, not only because she had got bored many nights and spent hours online shopping for clothes but because she liked to wear dresses when she could.

Not that she ever got the opportunity to where them. Alexis smiled although her thoughts were completely different. She wasn't sure if Vladimir would let her out shopping with other people, with humans when he wasn't there to protect her, or Caleb or Louie for that matter. She also wasn't sure that she would be allowed to attend parties or any kind of other school activities.

Vladimir had only said she was allowed to attend school, he was a man of his word and that was why he always watched exactly what he was saying.

Which normally crippled Alexis when she tried to look for loop holes, she was just going to have to talk to him and try and make it out to be a good idea. A social able idea that would benefit her and them in some way, although she was sure she could somehow get around it.. “Ah Marie. There you are!” Cassie turned around obviously looking out for Marie.

Alexis turned – although enjoying these new people that she met, if someone had another class the same as her she felt like she should focus on them. Cassie squealed and moved forward to greet her friend, pulling her into a hug. Alexis turned around with a smile on her face, she loved how humans reacted to one another and she couldn’t wait to join in on such a marvellous greeting.

When she felt more confident with them as friends. She would feel much better.

Almost instantly Alexis's face fell, her skin began to tingle and her hair stood on edge as if the hackles of a dog were raised. Alexis tried to hide her falter by smiling although she found it difficult. There wasn't just one werewolf in the school but now she had three, and two of them were standing right in front of her. She could feel it, she could smell it – as much as she wished she couldn't.

It felt like a ton of bricks weighing down on her. The two girls seemed to realise that she was a werewolf at the same point she realised they were.

They were complete opposites in every way, shape and form.

Marie was plump although very beautiful – Her skin was pale and her hair was light brown, thick and bushy, her eyes seemed to tint into a light hazel colour. The other werewolf was thin, tall and tanned. Her pupils were almost back and her hair matched that. It was long and thinly cut.

Marie seemed over joyed at Alexis's werewolf status, the other werewolf didn't look at all pleased – in fact more calculating. "Alexis this is Marie, she has the Language Class with you and so does Sandy" Cassie chimed in not seeming effected at all by what was going on in front of her, although Alexis noticed the slight change in her voice showing her displease with Sandy. She obviously didn't like the girl yet none of the two reacted to it.

Alexis wanted to say that humans were weird but considering they weren't '*all*' humans – she couldn't exactly say that. "Marie, Alexis. She is in most of my classes and I knew you took Languages Honours so I thought you could help her with that or at least show her where the class is considering she's new and all" Cassie spoke her usual sing-song voice as she pulled Marie into another hug, gently squeezing her before releasing her. Sandy stared on towards Alexis and the brunette tried her best to ignore the gaze which was becoming increasingly difficult. Alexis couldn't find the words to speak but she knew that wasn't going to be a problem with Cassie here beside her – she would always speak for her.

"That is no problem, Cassandra. I would more than happily take Ale-xis to her class. I believe we have it next anyway" Marie spoke with a little bit of a posh accent, her eyes staring off towards Alexis in amazement before returning to Cassie. "Because it's so difficult to find a classroom in this school" Sandy smirked at her comment, her eyes flashing with annoyance and her voice holding all of its arrogance.

Cassie stamped her foot drawing Alexis attention – Stunned; Alexis couldn't believe someone beside her actually stomped her foot in annoyance? She didn't think people actually did that. "Don't be so rude, Sandy" the red mane lion beside her acted like a diva who was not getting her way – a spoiled rich kid never the less but it couldn't help but make Alexis smile during the situation she was in. She was caught between her greatest fear and something she wanted after all.

This school contained werewolves; if Vladimir knew anything like that then he wouldn't allow her to come back. Ever.

Sandy finally took her gaze away from Alexis and sent an evil look Cassie's way which made the red head stumble slightly although she didn't back down. She opened her mouth to say something else and it was covered by a manly hand. "That will be enough from you, sweetheart. Let's get you to your next Class before you get yourself in to a fight" Chris pulled Cassie away from the small group, taking Alexis's only defence away from her. Cassie was dragged away and soon left the class with her friends completely forgetting about her fight with Sandy.

Alexis stood staring at the ground not knowing what to say, what to do. They couldn't very well do anything to her in a class that was busy, but they knew who she was now. They knew she was a werewolf. "Come on, we better get to class. Mr Miller hates it when we are late" Marie urged Alexis on taking a step towards her as if she was about to link her own arm through Alexis.

Automatically Alexis took a step back and Marie froze, surprised by her reaction momentarily before offering her a smile and waving her hand in the direction of the door. Alexis knew that the best thing she could do in this moment would be to go to class while the hall was still packed with students. She didn't want to be alone with these werewolves – not a chance.

Marie and Sandy turned to head out the door and Alexis moved to follow behind them.

12

Public enemy number one

Alexis had no choice but to follow them to her next class, she couldn't show them that she was scared; she couldn't just turn and run away from them. This was her only chance at being in a normal school and if there were only three werewolves in the full school it couldn't be that bad.

Could it? She had been living with vampires long enough to know how to avoid them, she could learn the same about werewolves. It wouldn't take her too long. Alexis could work around this. She had to stop in her steps before she hit one of the werewolves. Sandy had turned around to face her and now with a crooked smile on her face. "You're a werewolf" She pointed out in a matter of fact tone and Alexis couldn't help but laugh awkwardly; trying to cover up how she was feeling in that moment.

Trying to disguise everything and push the situation away from herself, she tried to seem distant about the subject. “Sandy, Sh” Marie tried to hush her friend but one look from Sandy shut her up. Sandy wasn’t going to take orders from Marie.

Alexis shook her head and moved to go past the werewolves in front of her, she felt like her full body was tensed up “Don’t be stupid there’s no such things as werewolves” Alexis held up her façade and walked around the wolves. She didn’t want to be anywhere near them and if she could avoid confrontation then that was what she was going to do. She walked around them and began to head along the corridor, pulling her timetable out of her pocket; she tried to find the room number stated on it. She heard a great distressing sigh come from behind her and then their footsteps followed her. “Avoid the question then weirdo” Sandy answered although she could hardly say that Alexis avoided the question, she answered just not the way Sandy wanted her too.

The girls moved to walk beside her, one on either side. Alexis's hairs stood on edge. She tried to put on a fake smile although it was hardly working. She was in the middle of two creatures she didn't want to be near. "I'm not avoiding anything, Sandy. I told you what I think" She shrugged her shoulders and crossing her hands across her chest. She was trying to make herself as small as possible and as thin as possible considering they were next to her.

Sandy had gathered herself back up and smiled sideways towards her. "I see. So your tails between your legs because you're scared?" Sandy sang out as if she was singing a dramatic ballad. Marie was walking a thin line - she knew there was something about this new girl that was tugging on her wolf; she just couldn't place what it was. So instead of doing anything she stayed silent beside her. Sandy would eventually tire; all she was doing was trying to prove she was on top. Marie knew she was on top, but Alexis didn't.

"Stop it" Alexis whispered very softly, she was shaking. She didn't want to be near any werewolves never mind having three in her school that she could bump into every day. Sandy sniggered slightly as the moved along the corridor. "The class is the last one on the left" Marie added in with a soft tone, she could feel Alexis's words echoing through her, feel them connect with her wolf, her wolf had quieted down within her. She felt confused but dare not question it.

Logic was telling her something was wrong, yet her need to survive was telling her to stay quiet, to not speak up and interrupt Sandy.

Sandy on the other hand wasn't stopping, she was enjoying herself. "Are we ruffling your fur?" she chuckled skipping along beside her as if she had nothing better to do. Marie was an omega within the werewolves, she knew her place and she always followed her orders. Sandy on the other hand knew nothing of the kind; she was born from a small beta family and always wanted to reach to be alpha material. She didn't know when to stop. "Don't worry I am sure a nice pet will always make you feel better"

Werewolves referring to themselves as dogs? Now Alexis had heard everything. She didn't want to react to her but at the same time she was itching to shout at her, to growl at her. *No*, she couldn't do that.

Alexis shook her head, she couldn't deal with this. She wouldn't deal with this. "Oh did I hit below the belt this time? You must be reacting to the moon tonight, don't worry it happens to all of us" Sandy kept on with the werewolves jokes, she was determined to break Alexis and she didn't care who she hurt in the meantime.

Marie shot a look towards Sandy although she ignored it. She wasn't going to listen to someone lower than her, she had worked hard to get higher up on the chain of command. She was the queen bee; she was dating the alpha's son. She couldn't get any higher up the chain than that. He was the next alpha and she was going to be his wife, his mate; nothing could stop that, nobody could.

Sandy seemed to chuckle when Alexis didn't react. She was obviously getting the reaction she wanted. "Don't worry we don't bite. Well not all of us anyway. Sometimes we nip but it's more playful than hurtful" Sandy was pushing her and somehow Alexis knew that she knew that. Alexis felt like she wanted to growl but like always she suppressed it. She would not give in to this force; she would not let those werewolves push her in to submission. She wasn't going to play the game they were playing. She wasn't going to sink to their level but she did need to stop them. She couldn't take any more of their jokes.

With the vampires it was one thing but with werewolves, well it seemed like a completely different situation. One she wasn't sure she could handle. She swallowed her growl and pushed out one word. "Stop"

This time without thinking her eyes narrowed and she let it slip out with more force than she had ever spoken to anyone with before. Both girls stopped in their tracks as Alexis continued on to the end of the hall.

They were stumped; neither of them wanted to but found themselves having to.

Sandy's mouth was left half opened staring at the girl. She realised straight away what she was now up against. She was up against an Alpha. A nature born Alpha.

Alexis walked to the end of the hall and turned towards the classroom, her eyes went straight to the girls still were she left them. Without a second thought the girls started moving and Alexis went into the classroom. As soon as she stepped through the classroom doors she took a deep breath and smiled towards the teacher.

"Ah our new student, Alex is it?" Alexis smiled and bounced her head into a nod. She didn't need to correct someone, she couldn't correct him. She had just told two werewolves to stop, she had shouted at two werewolves. She couldn't do that. She shouldn't have opened her mouth. That was going to come back and bite her; literally, from now on she needed to avoid the werewolves. She could find her own way about this school; even if she was late she could deal with that. "You can sit in the back there. We have one seat left just for you" He spoke clearly and with a strong English accent. *This was her language teacher?* A smile traced her lips as she sat up the back of the class. She took in a deep breath, her hands gripped her thighs as she worried about the back lash she was about to get.

The girls walked into the class one after another and to Alexis it seemed like it was in slow motion. First Marie walked through the floor, her head lowered and she moved straight into her seat in the second row, then Sandy followed, although she tried to hide the fact that her head was lowered and her ego was wounded, she sat down beside Marie. Alexis was safe for the time being – but she knew it was only because she was in a class with a teacher and another twenty pupils. Her mind raced through a million possibilities in her mind as the teacher began to start talking.

"In this class we are going to continue the languages on from the past years and add another one on. Which for our new student I will go over them. French, German, Italian, Chinese, Spanish and our new language Greek" A smile graced his lips and Alexis hands gripped the table in front of her as she reached into her bag and took out her notepad and pen. Her pen couldn't stand still – it tapped the paper as soon as she brought it out. "Now I completely understand if you aren't fluent in these languages but by the end of this year I want you to be able to have a full conversation in each language. We shall break each language into 8 week periods" Alexis could hear him speak and luckily she had already began learning the languages he was speaking about.

She was fluent in French, Russian, English and Italian although the others ones she would have to work on but she was willing to do that.

She was willing to work. But she couldn't work worrying about what these werewolves were going to do. She shook her head, she needed to focus. She couldn't spend her full school experience in fear. It wouldn't work; there would be no point in staying. She would be better giving in.

With a deep breath she threw the werewolves out of her thoughts and focused exactly on what the teacher was saying. She was going to enjoy and learn in the school environment. "Now let's start with Spanish – Who knows how they start a conversation in Spanish, Xavier?" The class moved into a discussion and when questioned she tried the best to answer every question directed at her without her voice wavering. As she began to get into the class she soon forgot about Sandy and Marie and began to enjoy the discussion and the class atmosphere.

It was all beginning to come together nicely. Or this class was anyway. She couldn't think about what would happen after the two hours. She just wanted to focus on her language class. She was good at learning and that was all thanks to Vladimir he had kept her learning from a young age – she was sure she could develop the languages in no time.

She was more interested to learn Greek and more than likely that would be the last one they would learn. She had to stick it out. It couldn't be that hard to ignore the werewolves in this school. She just had to work on staying away from them.

Focus on school. She warned herself.

13

It's a buffet!

Lunch.

That was what she had to deal with next. She had to eat like a normal human being in a room full of other humans. Except she couldn't step through the door to the lunch hall. Part of her told her she looked stupid just standing outside the lunch hall waiting on something or someone. She wasn't sure what, well actually she was. She wasn't waiting on anything; she was looking to see who was in the lunch hall.

But from this angle she wasn't getting a very good view on it. She could hardly see where anybody was, she could see a few tables of people she didn't know and where everyone got their lunch.

That was it. She let out a deep sigh and tried to move herself to see more. She didn't get to see anything more, Cassie's lion haired mane appeared at the window, and her face was glowing at the other side as she waved at Alexis before opening the door to question her. "You realise you have to come in to get the lunch, right?" Cassie questioned her hand rubbing her elbow as if in a nervous habit.

A smile formed on Alexis's face as she chuckled nervously. She knew exactly that, but she didn't want to go into the hall, not alone anyway. She couldn't face the three werewolves she knew were going to be in there. She had met them. She had avoided them as much as she could. But she couldn't very well stay out here all of lunch time – she was hungry after all.

So she did the only thing she knew would cover for it. She changed the subject.

"You said there was some kind of lunch system?" Alexis tried to cover what she was actually dealing with by using a real problem that was there. Not that she had even begun to think about that problem. *What did a lunch system even mean? Could you not get your lunch unless you knew how to work it?* The thought actually scared her as well, not as much as the other problem of course but never the less. A laugh echoed in Cassie's throat as she pulled Alexis through the door and began marching her towards the area with all the food.

It was drastically different than she imagined, not like any cafeteria she had seen in any movie. The tables were smaller and they all had people crowded at them, the food was spread out along and looked like they had taken care in making it. It looked more like a restaurant than a cafeteria for kids. "I'm sorry. I must have scared you to death with that lunch system nonsense. Don't worry it's just a card system we have here…" She pulled a card out her pocket and waved it in Alexis's face as if to show her exactly what she meant.

The quizzical look on Alexis's face told Cassie that she had no idea what she was talking about. "…You can use my card today and then tomorrow we can go and get you your own one.

Basically you put your money on the card at machine points around the school and they swipe your card as if it's a credit card. I always have mine stocked up. You can buy me lunch later…" She waved off any thought of Alexis rejecting her offer to buy her lunch and the lion haired girl couldn't help but make her smile with her over dramatic attitude. She stopped at the food station picking up two trays and sliding them in front of both herself and Alexis.

"Now just tell them what you want and they will put it on a plate for you. You get your meat choices here and then your starch stuff next – that's your chips, potatoes, rice and all the rest and then you get your fruit and veg. And lastly your chocolate and sweetie stuff you have to get on the other side of the room. I think they put it over there to stop people from buying it or try and detour you from doing it anyway. It doesn't even faze me. I need chocolate to make it through the rest of the day" Cassie admitted with a smile as she slivered along the lunch bars, pointing at the things she wanted.

Alexis followed suit, everything looked good, and there was a variety of meats – chicken in a choice of two sauces, sweet and sour or white wine sauce. Beef was also an option with gravy, and then there was lamb with mince sauce, pork with apple sauce and lastly corndogs. It was easy for Alexis to pick she had always had a lovely craving for pork and with the apple sauce she was more than happy to indulge in it. She moved through the rest of the menu, picking off the things she liked before they ended up at a till.

Cassie filled her plate to the brim and handed the women her card "Both these meals" she waved her hand over the meal she had created for herself and Alexis's meal and the lady typed in numbers to her till before swiping the card down the side of it and handing it back to Cassie.

Cassie pushed her card into her back pocket and lifted her tray up. "Come on. The guys always keep a seat for me and I asked them to keep one for you as well" Cassie beamed towards her waiting for Alexis to pick up her tray before she turned to walk beside her looking out for her friends. Alexis didn't want to look but couldn't find anywhere else to put her eyes too. She couldn't look at her tray – she didn't know if she would run into someone and end up spilling the tray over some unfortunate soul. She tried to look forward and she found herself searching for someone she knew.

Even though she didn't want to. She set her eyes on Sandy the moment a shiver ran up her spine. "There they are over there" Alexis's attention was gladly taken away from Sandy to look at where Cassie was pointing.

Where just like in home room, sat her group of friends with just like she promised two spare seats beside one another. Alexis felt herself tense up feeling eyes on her. She knew exactly who they were. Sandy's and right now she had her back to her as she turned around to go to her seat.

"There's the home schooled girl" the tall brunette head boy that she remembered Cassie saying he was called Chris and she offered him a smile as Cassie moved into the seat beside him and Alexis dropped in to the seat beside her. Her tray she pushed on to the table in front of her and when she looked forward she couldn't help but tense up a little bit more.

In front of her, was not just Sandy or the three werewolves she had met but a full table of werewolves. She counted five, although her brain was on overdrive so she wouldn't have doubted if she had missed someone. Sandy was there draped over a boy to her right, the boy was staring at her, his short spiked hair was neatly cut and not too short either.

Marie was beside Sandy on the other side, the boy she had ran into first was two away from Sandy on her right. He wasn't looking at her he was too busy talking to the other boy across the table beside Marie. They looked very similar in build; both had dirty blonde hair, with dark eyes.

Although the one beside Marie had slightly longer hair which was much like Caleb's style. They both had strong jaw bones and muscular arms. All the hairs on her body were on edge, her tongue snaked out licking her lips nervously and she was sure she looked like an awkward fool staring at them. "Off in your own world?" She came back to stare at the Blondie haired girl gazing at her with a smirk on her face, and her hand up as if she was about to wave it in Alexis face.

Alexis nodded sheepishly towards the girl she recognised as Ashley. “Sorry” She answered, starting to dig into her food. She needed a distraction and she needed one fast. The food on her plate was one she enjoyed and she knew right now it could distract even for a little while.

“There’s no need to be sorry Alexis. Ashley just likes to know what ever one is thinking, she can be nosey like that….just ignore her” A smile crossed the red haired girls lips as she stuck her tongue out towards Ashley. Alexis didn’t know how to react to what was happening; she switched her eyes towards Ashley as if waiting to see her react. Her nostrils flared and Alexis didn’t want to get into a fight on her first day, she felt herself shrinking down into her chair.

This couldn’t be happening, she thought the werewolves were the worst part of her day and now the humans were fighting? “Besides most of the time she’s off in her own world” Cassie added in which only seemed to entice her more. Her eyes lit up with the challenge and she disregarded her plate to the side to lean on the table. "Nosey? Miss Cassandra Goldfoot. You normally know every bit of gossip in this school before the newspaper does. You came into class already knowing half of Alex's life and you're going to call me nosey" She was ready and Alexis was shocked although it didn't seem to bypass Cassie, the two seemed to be so easily battering that Alexis didn't know when they were kidding or when they were going to be serious.

Was this a serious conversation? She was confused. "I will-…" Cassie started although Chris nudged beside her. "I think you're going to give Alexis a complex if you guys keep acting in this way. We may understand what you two always bicker about but if that isn't a confused look I don't know what is…." Chris answered and they all turned to look at Alexis. Her cheeks brightened and she slouched back into her seat a little bit more, not liking the idea of being stared at any more than the idea of being the centre of attention.

“You’ll honestly get used to them” the other boy, Jack spoke from beside her, he smiled towards her and Alexis smiled back. They all moved back into a much gentler conversation, occasionally asking Alexis question’s she was prepared to answer thanks to Vladimir and the backstory that they had prepared. They seemed like a nice bunch of people.

Normal, human people and that was what she needed. That was what she wanted, a smile lit her lips as she joined in to the conversation and tried to ignore the werewolves across the tables, she would have to ask Cassie who they were. But then again maybe it was better if she didn’t know who they were. She didn’t want to be the centre of their attention nor even near their attention. If she could stay out of their radar. Out of Sandy’s radar especially, then she would be more than happy.

14

Mine, Mihi

Sandy felt the growl in the back of her throat, although she tried to supress it, when she saw Alexis stride across the middle of the lunch hall with Cassie and sat directly across from them. The boy she was leaning on, Nicolas's body tensed full and she was sure that he had noticed her as well. She stared daggers into Alexis.

"Who is that?" she heard the words from beside her. Nicolas couldn't take his eyes from the girl, Alexis was staring right back at them. She was scared, they could all smell it.

They could sense it by the way she acted around them, that was one of the reasons Sandy had made sure to poke fun at her so many times. "I ran into her this morning – she's new here and a wolf, although she was surprised to see another wolf in the building. It was almost like she had expected us not to be here. Its common knowledge this is where our pack attends so I don't understand why she would be surprised" Alexander leaned on the table; he picked up his drink, having already scoffed his food. He didn't look over to where she was he didn't need to see her twice. He knew exactly who they were talking about after their interaction this morning.

Alexander was strong on his temper; he had anger problems and often had to be calmed down his best friend, the Alpha's son. Nicolas. Nicolas was interested because of one reason and one reason only. His wolf was scratching at him with one word and one word only.

MINE.

It was shouting at him as if it was going to rip him apart to get towards the other girl, his heart rate was picking up as her beautiful green eyes stared back at him. His thoughts were racing and there was one thing he was certain about, she was his mate. He visible moved to make sure he was further away from Sandy.

Sandy was shocked when he moved out of her grip to lean on the table to inquire more about this girl, his heart melted when she turned back to talk to the humans at the table, her smile nervous and awkward and her cheeks burning. He had never seen something so beautiful.

"What's her name?" He asked almost without thinking, to anyone and nobody in particular. Marie was the one to talk first knowing that Sandy wasn't going to talk up big, especially about Alexis after what had happened earlier. "Alexis. She's in our foreign language class and…" Marie glanced towards Sandy who was staring daggers at her, as if to warn her not to mention anything else. She knew Sandy didn't want to let them know what she was. "Yes?" Nicolas's attention pulled away from Alexis for the first time since she had come into the room.

His eyes piercing at Marie in questioning. There was one thing Marie was sure of and that was Nicolas was going to be alpha, not Sandy and she liked Nicolas, she wasn't going to start lying to him. She gathered up her courage, even letting her wolf rise to the surface a little as if to protect her.

Her eyes concentrating on Nicolas fully and not Sandy.

Although her voice stayed lowered. "…She's an alpha. There's no doubt about that and a strong one at that, if I didn't know any better I would say she was a Lupei. She told me and Sandy to stop and we froze, we couldn't move from the spot we were in. Our full body was against us for those few moments until she looked back at us. That's when we could move again" Marie knew what she was saying was crazy; the Lupei werewolves had been killed off completely when they were all pups.

They had only ever had experience with them once when they were watching videos and dvd's and of course what their elders told them. Marie knew only Lupei werewolves could have that much control over someone else's pack, because of her granddad. He was one of the last surviving pack elders. Her granddad was the pack's oldest Doctor and Marie was training to be one under him. She was proud to be. She often spent many weekends in the pack's surgery watching him treat the littlest things.

"You're kidding?" Alexander seemed serious as he stared at Marie as if trying to see if she was telling a lie. His eyes scanned over her in distrust. Patrick beside Marie sat up beside her, not liking the way his brother was challenging the girl beside him. It was, of course, his mate although they hadn't been open about it with other people.

Thanks to Patrick's and Alexander's father, he wouldn't accept someone unless they had a high level within the pack, which unfortunately for Patrick, Marie she was an omega and a very low one at that. So right now they had refused to tell anyone under agreement with each other. They had decided together that it was best to keep it a secret.

The older they got the harder it was to keep people from finding out though. It was hard to ignore that inner mate instinct. Nicolas was just finding that out.

Nicolas didn't seem interested in the bickering between the pack members he turned around to Sandy with the questioning look on his face. "Is that true?" He asked her a little more power in his voice since by the way she was sitting up proudly and trying to protect herself. He had to put power against his words if he expected her to tell him the truth, Sandy wanted to lie, she wanted to say it was a flock and they were just shocked that someone like that would answer her back but when she couldn't form the words she simply nodded her head. "We have to alert the elders if we think she is a Lupei, she's in danger if she is. There's no way that she's safe, there could be vampires anywhere in this city and they're not just going to let her by pass them quickly" Patrick spoke up trying to distract himself from Marie and focus on the problem at hand.

Nicolas nodded his head "We don't need to alert them yet. We can talk Alexis into coming herself I am sure. It'll be safer for her rather than the elders scaring her into coming" He said looking back over to where she was, her laugh echoed through him and he was sure he couldn't help but smile at it. "She's safe at home. She's been home schooled as far as I know. That was what Cassie told me. So obviously she was kept out of harm's way for long enough. I bet her parents are talking to your dad right now anyway, that's probably why she's been enrolled in this school, they must plan to join the pack" Marie spoke up with what she knew; hoping to make the up in coming Alpha less worried about the girl. She could see right away that he cared about her.

Sandy could as well.

She had almost let out a growl, as she folded her arms in front of her chest and curled herself up into a ball. "Probably" Nicolas mused as the bell rang overhead, telling them it was time to get back into class.

Everybody lifted their tray around the werewolves and moved to leave the hall, Nicolas's eyes were still on Alexis and when she lifted her tray, she was confused although followed Cassie's lead. Nicolas lifted as if to follow her but was stopped by a hand on his elbow. "Leave it Nic" Alexander spoke although Nicolas wasn't quiet registering everything at the moment.

Although Alexander's hand had at least stopped him from moving forward towards the new werewolf and when she left the room he was able to snap back into action. His eyes finally moved towards Alexander, nodding his head.

The chair rattling in towards the table beside him alerted his attention away from Alexander and towards Sandy; who had pushed the chair in hard against the table and stormed away from them, Marie smiled towards Patrick before going after her.

Although not before she picked up her tray and taking it with her to dispose of it before leaving the lunch hall with Sandy; who had decided to leave her tray on the table where she had been sitting. She had hardly touched her food.

The three boys stood staring as Marie and Sandy walked off. "That's going to cost you…big" Patrick was the first to break the silence as he turned around to face both his brother and Nicolas. A chuckle rumbled through him and his brother joined him after Nicolas's quizzical look. "Why?" he almost sounded stupid which was part of the reason why Patrick was laughing and definitely the reason why Alexander had joined in. "Are you kidding me?" Alexander spoke as he moved around the table grabbing not only his tray but Sandy's as well.

Both Nicolas and Patrick joined him. Alexander and Patrick looked at Nicolas as if he were crazy, he had to have known what he had done, sure none of them could normally understand what Sandy did but this time, they couldn't have missed it as if it were a brick smacking them in the face.

"Really? Nic? You looked like you were going to jump over the table and mount the new wolf in front of all the humans" A laugh came out of Alexander's lips as he scraped the leftover food on Sandy's plate into the bed before placing both his and her tray on top of the bin. Alexander was always blunt and would never beat around the bush. He would gladly tell Nicolas the truth, whether it was good or bad.

That was why he liked Alexander so much, which was why he had always been his beta. Nicolas automatically flinched not realising how obvious his attraction towards the new werewolf was. "Sandy isn't going to easily just forgive you this time. You basically pushed her away to get closer to Alexis" Patrick chimed in, as he nudged Nicolas pushing his tray on top and moving to hold the door open for them all. “She’s never going to be able to forgive me guys…” Nicolas started as he moved through the door; he was so sure about his next words that he knew it was going to anger Sandy.

Sandy had been his girlfriend for the 6 months, although Nicolas had known that she had admired him for longer than that. His dad wasn’t happy about him choosing someone like her to go out with but his dad had been certain that it was just a phase even though Nicolas had demanded it wasn’t and that he did love Sandy.

There was no doubt in his mind how he felt about her now. “Alexis is my mate” Patrick took in a deep breath in shock. Alexander stared at his best friend for a moment before questioning “Are you sure?” Although he knew Nicolas wouldn’t have said it unless it was true. Not a chance. Nicolas nodded his head and Alexander began to laugh. “Well good luck telling Sandy that. I don’t want to be you right now” Patrick joined in on the laugher nodding his head in agreement.

Nicolas knew how bad she was going to take it, although there was at least one thing he could be happy about. At least his dad would be happy. He would be more than happy that he was mated to another Alpha, but then again his dad had told him that he would be. That was one pointed he didn't like. His father was right.

He was never going to hear the end of this.

15

What's your point?

"Wasn't as bad as you thought it was. Right kid?" The driver turned towards her as she slunk in to the car, a smile creased her lips although she wasn't sure that she meant it. The man in front of her let out a laugh as he turned around and started up the engine. Alexis didn't know if it were bad or good.

It had been a mix of both; but she had this journey to change how she felt about that. She had to make Vladimir believe that it was the best thing she had ever been too. She had to lie to them or at least with hold the bad parts.

Otherwise he wouldn't let her come back; that much was obvious. She had to be careful, especially with someone

Vladimir had hired to take her to school. He either obviously trusted this man or could compel him completely without any outside influences; although Alexis had never seen this man before this morning she was sure that Vladimir would use someone he trusted. “It was great; just what I needed” Alexis smiled through her thoughts and pulled on her seat belt as the car pulled away from the school and started the short journey home.

The man tilted his rear view mirror so he could see Alexis in it. “Didn’t I tell you? I knew you’d enjoy it. All fun right? Did you learn a ton?” The man in the front inquired with a deep genuine smile and Alexis couldn’t help but feel bad for not being able to tell him the truth. Although she couldn’t tell him the whole truth. She had learned a lot in the classes she had attended and she had enjoyed them immensely.

The only part she had disliked had been the werewolves, and it was more the fact she had been terrified although reserved. They had noticed her as well and she was going to find it difficult staying away from them. She could use Cassie a lot though and the rest of the humans around her.

The werewolves never spoke to her in front to them – not fully anyway. She told the man everything about her work day – about her classes and how much she had enjoyed the school environment, she even couldn't help but mention Cassie in there and how bubbly she was and friendly.

Which was something Alexis had never had in her life, she had never had a proper friend. She had Vladimir and Louie, sure but other than that she had been stuck by herself. Well she had Caleb now although she wasn't sure what she could count him in yet, maybe he was in the same category as Vladimir and Louie.

He didn't seem like family – not in the same way they did. By the time the car had stopped, she had told the driver everything about her day – minus the werewolves of course and he had told her about some of his adventures during the day and a package that he had to deliver. "That's us here, Kid. I'll see you tomorrow" he killed the engine before turning around and producing a big smile towards her. "Thank you" he tipped his small bonnet towards her, dipping his head.

"My pleasure" Alexis grabbed her back when he finished speaking and undid her seat belt in the process, before she was slipping out the car and confronted by Vladimir. She shut the car behind her and pulled her bag on to him, she couldn't show any weakness and she couldn't think about anything that happened at school. She put on her best smile as he stood assessing her. "Hey chief. What's been happening here?" She beamed up towards him curious to hear what they had been doing all day and keep the conversation from her right now until she had a better control on her emotions.

Vladimir watched her for a moment before moving to the side to allow her to come in the house. "Louie has been …irritating. More than normal" Vladimir hissed out and his shoulders dropped as if in a shiver. Alexis stifled a laugh as she looked towards her father like figure and they began to walk through the house. Vladimir eyed her sideways and she shrugged her shoulders. "You said he was always irritating"

Alexis reminded Vladimir with a soft smile along her lips which he shook his head forward. "Yes but with Caleb here he has decided to be the torment of my life" Vladimir spoke with genuine concern and he seemed to be remembering a few of the events during the day, Alexis half wondered what they had gotten up to, what mischief they had caused to make Vladimir looked this…dishevelled. She had heard him moan before about how much a bane to his existence Louie was. Alexis also wondered how and why Vladimir had changed Louie in the first place and what had ever compelled him to do so.

Vladimir must have seen some quality he liked in Louie because surely he hadn't been made to change him. Alexis had always been so curious although had never asked; she was too scared for the answer and she felt it was too private for her to know. "How about your school life?" He changed the subject more concerned with her day.

Alexis shook out of her thoughts and looked towards him; the same smile she had placed on her face when her driver had asked appeared on her face again. "It was brilliant, slightly like how I imagined and slightly not" she beamed towards him and part of it was, part of her had enjoyed every minute of her chats with Cassie and her friends.

She enjoyed learning in a controlled environment and hearing other people's views on some of the subjects and not just her own and Vladimir's or even Louie's comments. It was thrilling to hear everyone debate a subject she enjoyed and even ones she had never heard of before. "I am learning a few more languages that could be useful and English was amazing, it's just great the way people interpret a story" Alexis wasn't lying in any sense, she had been impressed in the school because she hadn't expected people to have such vivid and open imagination.

"I have this girl, Cassie showing me around. I have never met someone so full of life. She's amazing and so full on. Do humans always bicker with each other?" Alexis was glad that they had surprised her, it almost made her feel more human the fact that they could think like her. Alexis was in amazement and she did enjoy school much more than she had ever expected too and she had expected to enjoy it.

She couldn't wait to go back, but reality hit her in face and she realised that she wasn't just going back to school; she was going back to the werewolves. "Yes" He answered with the nod of his head. She found herself coming back to reality and pulling her fake smile back along her face to look towards Vladimir. "I am glad you are enjoying it Alexis" He mused watching her for a minute more before turning to face the front.

"Have you got much homework?" His eyes looked towards her sideways before letting her lead them both up the stairs towards where their rooms were and also the room where Alexis had been studying in. Alexis shook her head "Nothing yet, although I want to keep up to date with everything and I want to reread, The Scarlet Letter, I need to take more notes on it and get more description out about it. They want us to discuss the character denotation and connotation in detail and I think I am missing something about Hester. We also have to discuss the themes and I know there are three obvious ones but I want to double check just in case I am missing some smaller ones"

Alexis smiled towards him and Vladimir analysed and listened to what she was saying just like he always did.

Both Vladimir and Louie had their good and bad points; and Vladimir's best point was his knowledge and what Alexis could learn from him, or what more Vladimir allowed her to learn from him. He always had a way of making her work it out for herself.

Which Alexis had grown to enjoy although hated as a child. "I can take a look over what you have got and see if you are missing anything important" Normally what would have been a question if anyone else had said it, but Alexis knew he was merely wanting to help her. She nodded her head "I have some notes in my room. If you can get the book and the rest in the study I can meet you there?" She inquired, unlike Vladimir who normally stated he would do things; Alexis still felt the need to ask things as questions. He nodded his head and disappeared along the hallway at a speed she was used too.

Alexis turned towards her room which wasn't far away from where she was standing, just a couple of doors down. Her door was shut just like she had left it; a smile lit her lips as she moved into her room. She knew exactly where she left the paper in her room; she hurried in through the door and straight towards the desk in her room.

Everything was filled neatly; she had acquired a touch of OCD and often had to have everything filled correctly. It made it that much easier to find. She got to her table and rummaged through the papers in the top of her filing shelves, knowing that she had put all her English work on top. Her hands filed through them although she couldn't find the piece she wanted, she couldn't find the title at the top of the page, the one she was looking for. "Where is it?" She whispered towards herself, scanning through the files again before looking to the next shelf. She had to have gotten mixed up although that wasn't something she had ever done with her paper work.

She didn't like sheets out of their place. "Do you always talk to yourself or is this a special occasion?" spinning around Alexis found herself staring at Caleb, sprawled out on her bed, one arm was stretched out behind his head the other was on his chest on top of a piece of paper and it was the second thing she noticed. She took a step forward towards the bed. “You have my work” She didn’t stop at a step she moved towards the bed before grabbing the paper out from under his hand and checking it to confirm it was the one she was looking for.

Scribbled at the top in her own hand writing was ‘*The Scarlet Letter*’, she looked towards Caleb accusingly. “What are you doing in my room Caleb?” She narrowed her eyes towards him in wonder now about why he had made his way into her room, surely Vladimir wouldn’t have let her walk in here without letting her know Caleb was in her room. Louie and Caleb were supposed to be at each other’s throat, Caleb was now sitting in her room and she was sure Louie would have normally been here to welcome her back. Yet he was nowhere to be seen. Caleb’s appearance had made her household act very strangely.

Caleb sat straight up on her bed and swung his legs so he was facing her. “How was your school day?” He ignored her question and Alexis rolled her eyes. Not the answer she was looking for in the slightest. She turned on her heels heading back towards her door. “It was good. I still have some work to do for tomorrow though” She spoke as she moved to the door, before she got to her bedroom door, Caleb was standing in front of her blocking her view. She looked up at him questioningly and when he didn’t speak, again she rolled her eyes.

“Cal. I need to get through the door” She didn’t try moving knowing that if he didn’t want to let her out of the room there was no way she could stop him. She had seen what he was like training and she knew the speed of a vampire and there was no comparison, especially when she had suppressed her werewolf gene. She stood no chance. He chuckled for a moment and Alexis looked up at him again with a questioning look. “Coming up with nicknames are we? I didn’t think we were that close…yet” Caleb took a step towards her and Alexis knew better than to back up from a vampire.

It was almost like a game to them, if she backed up it only meant that she wanted to play and right now, she didn’t want to play.

Plus Cal was better than some of the other names she had come up with in her head and none of them were particularly nice or polite. “What’s your point?” Alexis stared up at him refusing to be scared off by this new comer to her house. Especially one that seemed as bipolar as Caleb did.

Sometimes he could be an ass and other times he could care. It was like having Louie and Vladimir all wrapped up into one vampire. Caleb pushed off the wall shrugging his shoulders towards Alexis and letting her go through the door although she didn’t move. “I wanted to sort out a sort of training schedule so you could study around it.

Vladimir thought it would be a good idea so you didn’t try and do too much and get over tired. I know how much we can live more at night than during the day. Since you’re at school that probably wouldn’t work for you” Caleb wandered around her room, staring at everything as if it was highly interesting and Alexis’s eyes followed him.

“I was thinking 2 days a week, once at the weekend on Saturday which means we can do it more at night. Saves the hassle and the other during the week after you do homework say Wednesday?" Caleb turned on the edge of his feet, looking towards her for an answer. Alexis could see no problem with that. They normally did sleep most of the day anyway.

They were all up rather early today anyway but then again, that may have been because of Alexis being at school. She knew that. She bounced her head into a nod "Sure that sounds okay" Alexis agreed and Caleb smiled before striding towards her and the door.

A smile on his face once more. "Great we can start Wednesday night at about 8 then" he stopped short of her leaning to open up the door for her "Best get along to Vlad before he comes looking for you" Caleb edged her out of the door with his hand on her lower back, she let him and as she turned around to again inquire If that had been the reason for his intrusion into her room, he was gone. Vanished. Shaking her head and laughing towards herself.

Vampires. She thought, she couldn't help but feel like she was always stuck on a one sided conversation with them. She turned back and headed down the corridor towards Vladimir.

16

There's always a silver lining

"Alexis" her name was mumbled under someone's breath, it was low, deep but she was sure she recognised it. Her sleepy brain couldn't grip who it was though. "Mmhhh?" she grumbled out trying to come to grips with reality. *What time was it? Was it time for school?*

Her alarm hadn't woken her up. She was sure she would have heard its loud beeping. She was actually surprised that she didn't wake up the full household with its noise. But then again it seemed lately the household family just ignored what they wanted to hear. Alexis was beginning to believe that Vladimir and Louie's erratic behaviour was due to Caleb's timely arrival.

Not that she knew how to bring up the situation or even how to stop it.

“Get up” the voice was still hushed but this time it was closer. Alexis felt like rolling over and doing a very rude gesture towards the owner of that voice but held herself back knowing most vampires wouldn’t even flinch at the gesture she was thinking of.

And Alexis knew this was a vampire. In fact the closer the vampire was, the more she was beginning to understand exactly *which* vampire it was. She groaned at the thought of it. “I can get a pale of water over you in five seconds flat if that would help you up” the voice continued on with a slight amused sound towards it. Alexis wanted to do that gesture just a little bit more now.

She grunted and rolled over, pulling her hair away from her eyes to stare directly into Caleb’s blue ones. “What do *you* want?” she didn’t care that she sounded rude towards him, he was in her room, for the second time tonight and not only that she was pretty sure it was in the middle of the night. She had to be up for school in the morning and she didn’t think that any good could come from Caleb waking her up in the middle of the night. The vampire in front of her chuckled.

He threw a large clothed objected at her head and as she detangled it from her head she realised it was her dressing gown. "Put it on and follow me" the words were even more ominous that she expected them to be. She didn't think twice about it, her arms folded over her chest and she lifted her head defiantly towards him. "And if I don't?"

He didn't even flinch, his stride never faulted and he didn't turn back as he moved towards her door. "Then you miss out on it" was the last thing she heard as he walked out her bedroom door. *Dang!* He had hit her where it hurt – her curiosity. Now she was going to have to go out and see what it was.

What a jackass!

Alexis pushed herself out of her bed, pulled on her dressing gown with more effort than she needed; she grabbed her slippers and brushed down her hair before striding out of her door. She turned her head left and then right…there was no sign of him. "Caleb" she inquired hesitantly.

“Polo…” came his distant reply to the right. A smile crossed her lips at the stupid game he was playing before she turned and followed his reply. When she came to the end of the corridor there was two ways to go. Up or down.

This time she knew the game. “Marco?” she called out and let her ears open hoping to hear his voice closer this time. “..Polo...” It seemed the same distance away. She shook her head and turned to go up the stairs. When she got to the next level she paused for a moment, taking a look down the corridor. It was cold up here. She knew one of Vladimir’s offices were up – although she knew it wasn’t one he often used. There were piles of bedrooms which mostly stored nothing. *What possible need could Caleb have for taking her up here?*

“Marco?” she called out again staying at the top of the corridor. To her surprise the response didn’t come from the floor. “Polo” it came from upstairs.

Alexis was pretty sure there was nothing more upstairs. Apart from a locked door but still she ascended them and when it was clear Caleb was through the door, she pushed against it and it gave way. Slightly surprised that the door to the roof was unlocked she hesitated a moment before going through.

Caleb was standing on the roof. He was completely dressed in black, his low hanging jeans were held up by a black belt and his long sleeved shirt was opened slightly down his chest as he gazed up at the stars. "Aren't they beautiful?" he questioned after a long moment of silence. Alexis shook her mind free of the statement about how he was beautiful before following his gaze upwards.

What was he talking about? She wondered for a moment before she inquired out loud. "The Stars?" she asked without taking her eyes away from them. That was the only thing she could possible think he was talking about.

They were beautiful. She had never much spent much time looking up at the stars for all her years living in the night. She rushed about all night with Louie or played games with herself, or read a book but she had never just sat back and watched the stars. They *really* were beautiful. As if Caleb understood what she was talking about he didn't ask the question again.

In an instant he was at her side and her attention was back on him. He didn't say anything; he merely pushed her back further across the room until she was stood on top of a blanket. Which he lay down on. His ocean blue eyes stared up at her from their position "Lay with me?" the question hung on in the silence and his lips pursed as he waited for her answer.

He was serious, there was no playfulness in his tone like when they were training, and there were no secret cunning, dangerous eyes he normally stared at her with. He was being serious. After a moment of debating what he had planned she sat down beside him before laying back, her head beside his and her eyes cast up towards the heavens.

"I don't get you" She finally said, turning her head towards him. His eyes watched her closely and she could see his chest rumble with the chuckle that came out his mouth. "You're not supposed to get me" his answer held none of the answer she was looking for. Which she was sure was very intentional. She narrowed her eyes towards him.

He had wanted her to come out here. Perhaps if she threatened to leave he would finally tell her something. She doubted that would happen. “Why am I here?” she asked after a moments debate in her brain, which had started at standing up and marching away and finished with asking small questions to gain some insight in to her new bipolar vampire’s life. *Her?* Now she was the one talking crazy.

He rolled on to his side watching her for a moment. Contemplating something that Alexis couldn’t quite understand entirely. “You’re too curious for your own good” he replied his eyes never leaving hers.

She wanted to punch him.

In fact she wanted to do a whole lot more to him but punching him was one of the good ones. Of course she was curious. He had left her in her room, after waking her up with a really cryptic message about following him.

Any human, vampire or werewolf would have done the same.

She hoped they would have. Caleb had commented that her curiosity was one of her more human traits but Caleb’s curious nature had him following her around all the time and the werewolves at school were still stalking her so that seemed like it was also curiosity.

"You know curiosity killed that cat" he added in as an afterthought as his hand snaked its way over to stroke her hair. Alexis's eyes watched his hand and her heart rate picked up when he touched her hair. *What was he doing? What was she doing?* Alexis knew that he could hear her heart beat and yet she still allowed it to speed up. She wanted to curse herself but instead found herself biting her lip.

His eyes followed that moment, his eyes darkening. "I'm pretty sure it's Louie who killed my cat but then again Vladimir never liked it either" Alexis tried to lighten the mood slightly; she didn't like it when his eyes were black. Good things never happened when Caleb's eyes went black. He became moody and withdrawn. That was the last thing she wanted.

It seemed to work.

They were slowly returning to the blue and his lips quirked in a smile. "You had a cat?" her head nodded as she turned to look back towards the stars. “I asked them for a dog. Louie joked about wanting to be with my own ‘kind’ and I hit him repeatedly for it. So instead I asked Vladimir for a cat before I bought one next time Louie took me shopping” She turned her head back towards him as she watched his reaction.

He seemed amused by her story. “Vladimir blamed Louie. He kept repeating to him that he should never have let me near the pet shop and that Louie was the bane of his existence. Louie said that I pulled out the puppy dog eyes on him and that he couldn’t say no to me” A smile moved across Alexis’s face as she remembered exactly what had happened. “I told him I was going to teach the cat how to scratch him every time he made dog jokes. I managed to make it hiss at Louie every time he walked into a room” Caleb seemed to find this funny as well, his chuckle was warm against her ear, she hadn’t realised how close he was.

“Louie used to pick it up and take it to the trash can. I used to fish her out at least once a month and then suddenly she disappeared. Louie said he had nothing to do with it and

Vladimir said it was probably just hiding from Louie somewhere in the house but I never saw it again after that. We only had it a couple of months. Although I'm pretty sure Louie did something to her, or at least made her run away" Alexis shrugged her shoulders, she had speculated a lot about her cat but nothing had ever come from it. Louie hadn't talked about it – which to Alexis made him guiltier.

Caleb continued stroking her hair as if in a daze. "What was her name?" Alexis smiled. "Gem" she did actually miss Gem sometimes. The cat had stuck to her like glue the few months it was with her and she had enjoyed the company of someone other than the vampires in the house. She had talked to the cat, told it her secrets. It had been like a best friend.

Caleb's look was dazed. "My sister was called Gem" he said almost distracted, Alexis had never heard him talk about his family, she wanted to know. She needed to know. Something about Caleb having a family just made him more human to her.

She knew he definitely wasn't human.

But his family had been. “What was she like?” Alexis inquired with a soft voice, she felt like she was talking to her cat again. She didn’t want to scare him off; she didn’t want him closing up on her so she was trying to be as gentle and as soft as possible. “Childish, quiet and stubborn. She would always dress up and put on our mother’s make up. She would try to act as old as her as well. She pretended she was in charge whenever they went out. My older sister hated it but me and my brothers enjoyed it” Caleb spoke with a small smile on his face, one that Alexis had never seen before.

She found herself shifting on to her hip, so that she faced him completely, she placed her arm under her head as she got into a comfortable position.

“You had a big family” Alexis smiled slightly; she had never imagined Caleb having a big family. He seemed like the spoiled child sometimes which normally suggested someone was an only child. She had only made guesses of course about his life. That had been one of them. “Hmm” he answered her, his hand still stroking her hair ever so gentle.

He was lost in his thoughts, Alexis could see that. She wanted to know what he was thinking; she would have given anything to be in his head in those moments. "What were your brothers like?" she asked hoping to learn something else about him that she didn't know.

His shoulders shrugged slightly "Normal boys. We wrestled all the time. I was the oldest. The other two were twins. Christopher and Liam. They used to drag me around and ask me to play games with them. They always tried to ask me questions. "Who's tallest Caleb?", "Who's feet are biggest Caleb/" and "Who's the oldest Caleb?". I remember I always had to tell them they were exactly the same. My father constantly reminded me that. He told me that I had to always make sure I never favoured one over the other" He laughed at something and Alexis smiled towards him. He looked beautiful when he smiled but he looked gorgeous when he laughed. His blue eyes danced with mischief.

"When I started dating girls they always pretended to ask them questions. It was silly childish things but the girls ate it up. "Do you love my big brother?", "Are you going to marry him?".

I remember one time this girl mixed up their names repeatedly, and Christopher point blank turned around to me and said. “I don’t like her. Liam show her the door” and then Liam began to push her out of the door. I didn’t know what to do so I just waved and told her I would see her later” His eyes crinkled at the side and for a moment he stared at Alexis.

He was watching her reaction, she actually felt jealous. *How could she feel jealous? And what exactly was she jealous of?* Part of her wanted to believe it was because of the family life that Caleb had lived. The brothers and the sisters who he had grown up with. Alexis had none of that, she had often had to make up games by herself or play with items not people. Or Louie. But never had she had family like he had.

Another part of her believed that she was jealous because he was talking about other girls.

But that was a very small part of her. “Do you miss them?” her voice was soft, whisper like and she thought she saw his head nod but other than that he gave no other answer.

“I really don’t get you” Alexis said after another long silence, which made Caleb chuckle. Caleb leaned closer his lips gently brushed against Alexis’s cheek although not quiet in a kiss manner.

His breath was warm and she was sure she held her breath for the few seconds he was there. “I have another story for you. My mother used to tell me it when I started leaving the house a lot” Caleb was close and Alexis had the fight the urge to touch him. She hadn’t moved from her turned position but in her view she could see Caleb’s chest and his arm which was holding up just up beside her cheek, close to her ear. “One time an Angel seduced a Demon and it didn’t end well for either of them. She always reminded me to be careful. She always thought of me to be the Angel of the story, not the Demon” Alexis could feel his smile against her face. Her heart rate only increased and she felt flushed, her body heating up and she reached out to touch him. Her hand was against his arm.

“She always thought that I would end up seducing someone who would destroy me as I destroyed them. I always laughed at it. Especially the part about me being an Angel. But in reality I think it's a very accurate description" *Or what?* She had thought she had asked the question out loud but her mouth was dry and although she could have mouthed the words she couldn't find the words to speak.

He sat back beside her, his smile was darkened, and his eyes had changed as well. Alexis was sure that had happened when he was sitting back. She steeled herself for the darker Caleb.

She wouldn't let him annoy her.

His smile never faulted. "You should probably get back to bed before school starts. Wouldn't want you falling asleep up here" Alexis nodded her head and after a moment she left Caleb on the roof alone.

She really didn't want to leave him up there.

But it was clear she had been left with no other option. Caleb was a force to be reckoned with and when his eyes were black, Alexis didn't want to be anywhere near him.

17

Don't push me

The blood was boiling through Sandy; she was not going to give up. She was not going to let some *other* wolf come in and take away all the hard work that she had went through to get to the place she was. Sure, Sandy hadn't come from a completely Omega family not like was her friend Marie had. Marie enjoyed her status and she really didn't want to be anything more. Her father was a Beta, and she had always strived to be better.

It had been drilled into her from being a little girl by her mother. Her mother had been an omega before she had moved up through the ranks and took on a Beta. Sandy wanted to do one better and snatch the Alpha. She thought she had done it as well; she had Nicolas right where she wanted him. He would do anything she said, he would fetch her things and even when they were together things could be heated.

Which was exactly how Sandy had liked things, they had only been officially together for 6 months and Sandy had known that his father disagreed with their union although he proceed to let them be together which just meant that Sandy could work on him more, make him want her more and make it so that Nicolas couldn't live without her.

Which she thought had worked.

But it was now all being kicked off – all her hard work had crashed to the ground because of that *she* wolf. Sandy felt herself growl as she stormed through the corridors of the school. She knew it wasn't the best idea to confront Nicolas in school especially when she was this angry.

Emotions were one of the things that fuelled the wolves within them and Sandy's was scratching at the surface; ready for a fight although Nicolas wasn't the one she wanted to fight with. Alexis was. But right now she was going to settle with confronting Nicolas and hearing what he had to say about his behaviour. No one bothered her as she moved through the hallway, she had a determined walk and even when Marie saw her, she backed away and decided against talking to the angry wolf.

When she spotted Nicolas he was stood against his locker with Alexander beside him. His back towards Sandy, she didn't even think twice as she marched towards the pair. Almost instantly Alexander's head lifted up as if to defend his alpha and realising who it was, he gave a worried smile towards his friend. "Nicolas I need to talk to you" Sandy almost growled through her teeth, the alpha wolf turned although kept his back against the locker.

Alexander whistled as if trying to cover for the awkwardness he felt from being there with the two of them. "I'll catch you in class Nic." He said before turning around and leaving the pair to bickering, after all – Nicolas had already explained to them about the situation.

They knew why Nicolas had acted the way he had and he had already said that he needed to talk to Sandy about it. He had hoped to do it within the pack territory to keep Alexis safe and also to keep Sandy's anger away from the humans.

Nicolas hadn't the courage to tell her last night and when he had tried to find her, it seemed she had disappeared off running. His head had been spinning with thoughts of Alexis and he couldn't have concentrated on talking to Sandy at that moment anyway. So he was happy for the night to rest, but now he was regretting it. He should have done it within pack territory.

"I need to talk to you to Sandy, although this isn't the best place to do it in" Nicolas nodded his head, folding his arms in front of his chest and he repositioned himself in more of an alpha order. Sandy noticed his movements and growled in response even though she could feel her wolf backing down at his order. She was not going to give in so easily. She was going to stand up for herself.

When Nicolas opened his mouth up to speak, Sandy held her hand up making sure that she was going to get her words in first.

"I am not going to be treated like some second class citizen in our territory. I don't care if your alpha's instincts smelt another girl. I deserve to be treated properly especially if I am going to be your mate. We have fought to be together for a long time and I will not be pushed out of the way by some *she* wolf who's scared of her own shadow" Sandy felt like she wanted to growl at Alexis and in fact she would have fought to the death with her at any given point. She had ignored the second part of Nicolas's statement determined to get what she wanted to say out.

Sandy didn't think she was an alpha by any means, she was sure that the only reason they had stopped was because Sandy had been surprised by the fact that someone like her would talk back to her. That was what she wanted to believe anyway. She was making herself believe that.

Nicolas wanted to growl in return against Sandy, Alexis was *his* mate and he didn't appreciate anyone talking about her and since he could feel the hatred rolling off of Sandy – it made the wolf inside him pace, he could feel it coming up and against his eyes trying to make Sandy intimidated.

Nicolas knew he had to take it easier though; he hadn't wanted to hurt Sandy and he knew now why his father had felt sympathy for him over the fact that Sandy wasn't his mate. Nicolas had never expected to find his mate – even if his father had assured him that every alpha wolf did. He remembered his father's words so well *'It's just part of nature's way to make sure every alpha wolf is continued on'* Nicolas had nodded his head and thought his dad was just trying to scare him out of dating Sandy.

Of course Nicolas had dated girls before but none that he had went to his father about. None that he had thought would be his mate. He had thought he had wanted to be with Sandy, although now it seemed like a stupid idea. Now it seemed like he hadn't even known what he was thinking.

Which did make him feel a little bit guilt towards Sandy. His head shook towards her words. "I'm sorry Sandy…." Nicolas started and he saw Sandy smile slightly, not the reaction he wanted from her. "I didn't think you would apologise so easily for your mistake but I am glad you see you have done wrong here and I don't expect to see you doing it again. I mean don't get me wrong I don't mind you checking out other girls but that reaction was just too much for me" Sandy laugh moving her hand to touch Nicolas in which he moved out of her grasp automatically, her lips switched to a frown

"Wha-" Sandy stated to question him and this time Nicolas held his hand up towards her knowing it was the only way he was going to get time to speak. "Now I know you're not going to like what I have to say right now. I don't really like saying it to you either. But it has to be said….so here goes…" Nicolas took a deep breath, he had thought about what he was going to say to her for a long time and he knew each time he thought about it, it got harder.

Which only made him worry more, he had to tell her, if he was going to have any chance in speaking to Alexis and telling her the truth he first had to get through telling Sandy the truth. "…My reaction yesterday wasn't for nothing. I can't help how my body reacts to Alexis and neither can I help my wolf. Now before you interrupt me I need you to listen out and not speak. I know what I said to you over the past year and believe me if I knew what would have happened now I wouldn't have started us. I don't regret being with you at all of course we have had times that I will never forget but Alexis is something different, she is something I never thought I would have. She's my....-" Nicolas had nearly finished his speech, he had drifted off slightly thinking about Alexis. Sandy had notice how he spoke about Alexis and reacted accordingly, she had slapped him.

Nicolas's face stung and he could feel her hand vibrate off of him, he hadn't ever thought someone would have slapped him well enough Sandy. There were many things he had expected the young wolf to do and this certainly wasn't this. His hand automatically moved to cover his cheek which was now reddening from where Sandy had slapped him. He stared at Sandy in shock, she was furious; the steam was almost coming out her ears. Nicolas could see her wolf right through her eyes growling at him and he was surprised that wolf had allowed her to slap an alpha.

She was breathing heavily and he could see she was sweating slightly. She looked like she was holding herself back from changing and Nicolas became worried about the safety of his pack. *Would Sandy actually change and jeopardise that?* Sandy stood with her legs slightly parted and her fists clenched tight by her side.

"No!" She screamed towards him and Nicolas's eyes darted around lucky that no one was in the corridor around them. Everybody had cleared out no doubt when Sandy had started this conversation; the feelings rolling off of her would have scared anyone away. Nicolas reached his hands out towards her "Calm down Sandy" trying to make sure that she wouldn't let her wolf out. It was his job as the future alpha to make sure the protection of the species was intact and right now it wasn't intact.

Sandy was shaking with anger. "This is not happening. I have worked too hard to just be pushed aside because of some girl who is terrified of her own species…" Sandy snickered evilly towards Nicolas and his eyebrows rose in question. She decided to hop on his surprise. "...You didn't know? Well of course not you were too busy staring at her and Marie was too busy telling you all the good stuff. She may be a wolf but it isn't even close to the surface and if you can't see that then you're an idiot. She's not going to be part of my pack; I will not allow her to step in here…" Sandy was hushed by Nicolas look of utter disgusted, he growled towards her and Sandy automatically shrunk back although he kept a grip on her shoulders not allowing her to move any further back. "Don't push me Sandy. She is my mate and you do not get a decision on who joins *my* pack. You are not the alpha and you never will be with your attitude towards things. If she is scared it's because wolves like you have made her that way and I will make sure to show her that we are not all like that. You will not threaten nor search her out for a confrontation…do I make myself clear" Nicolas knew when he had stepped over the line, he knew when he had lost control and he knew exactly when Sandy had pushed him too far.

He hadn't meant to go all Alpha on her and he surely hadn't expected her to snap. She seemed to have snapped back to normal and her wolf had calmed down. Sandy's head stood strong and she almost refused to nod.

Almost. Nicolas let go of her arms even though she hadn't agreed to his demands yet and she reached her hands up and rubbed where he had held her so tightly although still she didn't agree with his demands. Nicolas was not going to let any harm come to *his* mate and he knew that a major threat would more than likely be Sandy and her hot headed temper. "She's not your mate Nicolas. Just because she's the first wolf to come along and look like she's a damsel in distress just means your alpha wolves are kicking in to save the poor girl" Sandy crossed her arms on her chest. *She was really going to do this?*

Nicolas stood his ground and shook his head against her words "I'm sorry you think that Sandy but you need to understand that it's not that. She is my mate. She is the one I am supposed to be with and nothing you can say will change that fact" Nicolas had calmed himself down as well and gained control over his own emotions and his own wolf.

His wolf hadn't liked being disobeyed like that. Tut-ting Sandy wasn't going to agree with him and Nicolas felt his wolf growl in response to her disobedience towards him. "..I don't think so Nicolas. But you can have your fun and we'll just see who-.." Sandy's head turned and Nicolas's eyes shot up just in time to see Alexis come around the corner.

Alexis hadn't noticed them, although she had heard their voices. She felt like a deer caught in head lights. She froze at the sight of them and Nicolas offered her a small smile, Sandy on the other hand wasn't happy, not in the slightest. She looked like she was ready to lash out at her. "Alexis" Nicolas breathed out her name and she felt a shiver run across her spine as she started to back away from the wolves in front of her.

Not saying a word. Sandy did growl this time and took a step towards Alexis. Alexis found herself backing up more quickly and when sandy took another step towards her she turned and ran up the nearest set of stairs, her heart racing out of her chest.

Nicolas had leaned forward and grabbed Sandy around the waist pulling back towards him. "I don't think so Sandy. Now Promise me or I will make sure that you don't" He growled in her ear, Sandy nodded her head towards them and he growled again wanting her to answer.

"I won't search her out okay" Sandy answered back in defeat before Nicolas let her go with a nod of her head obviously assessing the situation and realising that the situation wasn't going to get any better. Nicolas gave her once last look before going forward and seeing if he could catch up with Alexis.

18

Welcoming Committee

Alexis didn't want to get into any confrontation especially NOT with werewolves.

When Sandy had growled towards her and began to head her way she had felt herself tense up and she could have sworn the fear was rolling away from her. From that point on she wanted to make sure that she didn't run into any werewolves for a while.

Which was what she had done for the past two weeks, apart from seeing Sandy and Marie in her Foreign Language class. She had avoided going for lunch and instead and started to bring food with her, insisting that Vladimir go shopping because she didn't really like the food in school.

Which although he had rolled his eyes at and commented that sometimes people didn't get to choose what they eat and they just had to put up with – he still went and bought in a ton of shopping. She found the perfect spot outside and after a few days of not turning up in the lunch hall Cassie had questioned her about where she was going and then eventually came out with her to lunch.

Although she had still gotten food from the cafeteria and every so often she would bring two desserts out so that Alexis could have a special treat.

Cassie was beginning to be a great friend and someone that Alexis enjoyed being around. It was obvious that her and Chris were in fact a couple although none of the rest of the group seemed to be in a relationship with each other. Ashley was in a relationship with one of the boys that played American football though. Which Alexis had listened to the stories about him and smiled along with Katie and Ashley.

For two weeks she had successfully avoided the wolves. Alexis had almost enjoyed the peace she had, she believed that she was actually getting used to school and enjoying her time with her new human friends. It made her feel normal, at peace, human almost. If she didn't have the itching at the back of her head and have to go back to a home full of vampires she would have felt human.

Today though felt different; something was following her, someone was following her.

Alexis grabbed her bag a little bit tighter towards her shoulder and she moved along the empty hallway. She had gathered enough knowledge to know that she could get to most places once the coast was clear and every one was already in classes or nearly in their class. That didn't seem to have worked today. *Were they following her?* She felt eyes on her and she couldn't stop herself from searching around her with her blue eyes. She felt anxious. She powered on through the hallway, trying to remember which class she was supposed to be in.

The stress was rumbling through her and she couldn't think what class she was supposed to be in. She looked behind her, her curiosity getting the better of her. There was someone following her, although she couldn't see him. She could feel the fear creeping out of her. Alexis turned back around from walking backwards and stopped before banging into the person in front of her.

A Werewolf. Not just any werewolf. It was the one she had seen in the canteen with Sandy. "Hey" his chest rumbled and Alexis had to swallow the lump in her throat as she stared up at the wolf in front of her. She could feel the scratching at the back of her head again and she inwardly cursed – almost instantly it vanished. Her mouth went dry and she lost the words to speak.

"My names Nicolas, I'm the resident alpha's son here and I know you have had some trouble with some of the female wolves here but I want to make sure you know they're harmless and just surprised to see another wolf here; that is not within the pack" Nicolas's smile seemed genuine although Alexis couldn't completely take it in. She was sure that she was speechless in front of the tall male in front of her, her mouth opened and then closed a few times before she tried to look somewhere else.

Nicolas captured her chin in her hand and Alexis pulled her head away from his grasp, *why was he touching her?*

Alexis began to back away a little bit and found her back hitting something. She instantly turned around to see another werewolf. The angry one she had met first and she instantly took a step towards Nicolas without any thought. “This is Alex. He’s not as bad as he looks” Nicolas teased touching her shoulder and her eyes flew to him. “What do you want?” Her lips quivered as she tried to keep her eyes trained on both of them.

Although it was hard to do. Nicolas frowned and Alex merely looked at her in question. “We don’t want anything from you. We just want to welcome you in - this is the first chance we’ve been able to get you alone without mentioning to Cassie or any other humans the ‘W’ word.” Nicolas’s head turned to the side watching her; she put her back to the wall although it didn’t give her any less fear. Nicolas noticed her eyes switching between Alexander and himself and he settled his gaze towards Alex. “Alex, check the perimeter for me” Nicolas knew Alex was making Alexis nervous.

Alex took one last glance at his Alpha and the female beside him before nodding his head and turning away from him. Alexis watched him leave before her eyes were trained back on Nicolas. “Now is that a little better for you?” He questioned and although she didn’t want to answer, she found herself nodding in return.

It had in fact made her feel a little bit better, Alex had scared her that first day and he was a big werewolf who she wasn’t sure about. Part of her was afraid that he was just going to flip out and turn into a werewolf. *But then again didn’t she feel the same about Nicolas?* She was sure she did although he made her less nervous than the other werewolf.

“Your Alexis right?” he questioned as if egging her to talk. “That’s right” Alexis wet her lips finally finding the courage to talk, Nicolas’s eyes followed her tongue along her lips and he could feel the wolf inside him pacing, his full body felt on edge and on fire. His wolf was scratching at the bit whispering towards him just one word.

Mate. Her reaction though was one of fear and he could smell it, he did not want to scare her away so instead he knew he had to take it easy. "What are you so scared of?" Nicolas inquired surprising Alexis, she looked at him in wonder, his lips were slightly parted and although he had muscles he wasn't as tall and intimidating as what Alex was. He didn't seem as bad as what she had been told but then again what did she know about him?

Nothing.

She shook her head about to answer him back "You can't say you're not scared. I can smell it" Nicolas answered back folding his arms in front of his chest as he stared quizzically back at her. Just like vampires. When she didn't speak up he knew he had to cover the silence. "You're a wolf Lexi, you shouldn't be scared of any other wolf no matter what you have been through" Nicolas tried comforting her with his words but in fact the words were not comforting in the slightest. She didn't want to be near any werewolves and it wasn't because of her personal experience with them – well not really unless you counted when she was younger.

Which she couldn't remember anything about but she knew from Vladimir and Daniel that they hadn't been all good experiences. If it hadn't been for those vampires then she would have been dead. She was happy that they had saved her. She wanted to stand up strong beside this wolf but couldn't find the nerve to anymore. Nicolas looked concerned for her, although she didn't understand why. He didn't need to be concerned about her; he had no reason to be. "Where are you from?" Nicolas questioned her and she looked up at him, he was about a head taller than her. *But why was he asking her these questions? What did it matter who she was or where she was from?*

Nicolas caught her quizzical look and couldn't help but chuckle slightly. "You look so confused, its quiet cute" his words came out shocking her, making her look even more confused. *He was calling her cute? A werewolf – an Alpha werewolf was calling her cute?* She didn't understand what was happening. She slid slightly more away from him, the distance making her feel a little bit safer. "I don't understand" The words came out of her mouth although she didn't really understand them. She didn't understand Nicolas. Nicolas took another step towards her, matching her distance.

"What don't you understand?" Nicolas inquired, his eyebrows raised in questioning at her and to Alexis he did seem genuine. Alexis felt confused and that was the only start of her feelings. She bit her lip and she could see his eyes follow it. His eyes followed every small moment she did and she couldn't help but notice that as well. Her eyes followed every small movement he did, *why?* She wasn't sure. She didn't understand and that made things worse. "You" She stated simply looking up at him, she couldn't feel the scratching in her head any more, and she had pushed it down far enough.

But that didn't mean she couldn't feel his wolf. His body faced her and his arms were open by his sides, as if trying to be completely open with her.

Which was why she didn't understand him. The wolves she had met hadn't wanted to introduce themselves, they had intimated her, wanted to push her to be something she wasn't. Nicolas wasn't doing that. He was taking care with her.

Nicolas watched her intently. “You don’t understand me?” A laugh echoed through his mouth and a smile creased along his lips “What part of me don’t you understand? I’ll be happy to straighten everything out” Alexis couldn’t understand what needed straightened out, he was a wolf and she had been told wolves were dangerous, Nicolas didn’t seem particularly dangerous and for some reason she felt like she could trust him. “Wolves are dangerous” She blurted out hoping to assess his reaction, his eyebrows lifted slightly in questioning although he didn’t say anything waiting for her to continue,

Since part of him was scared she was going to close up on him again. He had just begun to get her talking. “Alex was the first wolf I met” Alexis stated and Nicolas couldn’t help but shake his head, a smile still appeared on his face.

“Unfortunately, Alex has anger problems. Just like any human would but because he’s a wolf it comes out a lot worse…” Nicolas shrugged as if trying to account for his fellow wolves actions and that brought a small smile towards Alexis’s face before she was shaking her head. Protecting his wolves sounded just like what an alpha would do. "No you don't understand Alex is the first wolf I have met ever"

Now that surprised Nicolas, his mouth opened and closed a few times, trying to find the words to say to her. It was Alexis's turn to raise her eyebrows; *Nicolas had never met a lone wolf? He had never met a wolf that wasn't in a pack?*

Alexis had thought that many wolves must have been loners, considering how Daniel and Vladimir had mentioned them. But then again there were many things not adding up in this situation. "…And then Sandy antagonised me, which was the second wolf I met. Marie wasn't as bad but she didn't help nor try to stop Sandy either…" Alexis went on, looking at his face, watching his reaction. None of his *'packs'* movements had seemed like a welcoming gesture.

None had made her feel welcomed. She felt more isolated and part of It was why she was so confused. Alex and Sandy, even Marie pushed forward and made Vladimir's stories real – they looked out for themselves and they intimated others, Sandy had even made a go for her last time they had met.

Now that didn't seem like a perfectly welcoming pack. Even Nicolas and Alex had hunted her down and followed her, making her more scared. But Nicolas's voice, his words, his attitude, contradicted that. That was why she was confused.

Was he playing some act? Was this a game to them? Alexis had thought they would have become bored by now; she had been in this school for three weeks now. Two of those weeks she had successfully avoided them – even in classes she had avoided them, stayed away from them, ignored their looks, even shut her ears and tried to ignore them speaking.

Nicolas's hand stretched back over his neck awkwardly scratching there, his eyes looked over her and his lips quirked in a half smile, as if he were sorry for that. "I can see your point. Alex is just – well Alex and Sandy just does not enjoy any females company, she tolerates Marie because Marie does what she wants but within the pack, she doesn't talk to any other female, she always has. It's like she feels intimated by them and well she feels intimated by you for a number of reasons" Nicolas shrugged; the words he spoke about Sandy were very ominous.

They left a lot to think about, Nicolas was watching her with his big brown puppy dog eyes and she was sure that he wanted to say something else, but he was holding back. *What did he want to say?* Alexis stared at him as if waiting for him to continue.

Although he had explained the reason for the way they acted the fact was it still didn't change her thoughts about wolves. "When was the last time you ran?" Nicolas questioned as Alexis came out of her day dream, she looked at him in wonder, *when was the last time she ran?*

It took a moment for it to click what he was really meaning he was meaning as a wolf. Alexis shook her head and shrugged towards him, her eyes searching everywhere but at him. "Now you're being the one confusing, you're wolf must be scratching at you like mad if you haven't let it out in a while" Nicolas smiled and spoke as if it was an everyday conversation. Which to Alexis it was far from it; she had never spoken to anyone about this kind of stuff. She had basically ignored it from the moment she had locked it away.

Alexis needed to get away now, it had felt nice talking to Nicolas but that didn't mean she wanted to continue doing it. "I really need to go I have a class" Alexis moved to go past Nicolas but was stopped by his arm on her shoulder, it was gentle. She finally looked back up towards his eyes questioningly. "You're not alone here, Lexi. I don't want you to feel like you have to avoid us. Alex is going to try harder, and Sandy won't be near you – she has been warned" Nicolas answered, his eyes looked at her expectantly and Alexis squirmed under his gaze nodding her head and trying to move away.

"I'll walk you to your next class" Nicolas spoke up, his smile still on his face as he let go of her shoulder and moved to walk beside her. Alexis started to walk and so did he. "You really don't need to walk me" Alexis gripped her bag to herself a little tighter, she kept her eyes trained forward and tried to keep a small distance away from him.

Nicolas walked with a small sway, his arms swinging by his side. A laugh echoed in his throat and he nodded his head "Yes I do" Alexis wasn't sure what else to say to that, he was confident and wore a deep smile. He was attractive, kind but strangely alluring – with other werewolves she wanted to turn and run but with Nicolas for some reason it seemed different.

A smile lit along her lips at the fact he thought he had to walk her but the words that slipped out her lips contradicted it. "Why?" They were getting close to Alexis's class, slipping up the stairs and without as much stress as before, Alexis knew what class she had. *College Prep.*

But what came past Nicolas's lips was something she didn't expect.

It was something she was sure – not even he expected to tell her yet. "Because you're my mate" the words had Alexis stopping in her tracks and when Nicolas realised what he had said, he stopped and inwardly cursed.

That wasn't what he was supposed to tell her; he was hoping to break her into it – he hadn't expected to feel so comfortable around her and it felt natural for him to be around her. It felt so natural to say those words out loud. Which was stupid on his part, he should have been concentrating more instead of enjoying the moment. “What?” Alexis felt her voice rise slightly and she instinctively moved around and away from him.

Nicolas held out his hands feel like an idiot and that he had just lost her. “I…Lexi. I just….” He couldn’t find the words to say, he wanted to make her feel better but he couldn’t lie to her and say he didn’t mean it. “Look Nico I really need to go.” Alexis was nearly at her class and she was glad to be able to disappear into it. She tried to smile towards him although it didn’t come across as a smile; it more so came across as if she was scared. “Thanks for walking me” She moved along the corridor quicker than she had before, her feet tapped the ground. Nicolas voice was there just before she lost herself in her class. “Lex”

19

Tension Training

This was not happening.

Alexis had spent hours on the computer in the study researching words and what they could mean but when it came to werewolves and their *mate* there was only one meaning for that. Alexis was determined that she wasn't a werewolf's mate, not even to one as nice as Nico was. She shook her head to both the thought of his nickname in her head and that he was nice. His name was Nicolas and he was a werewolf. She wasn't safe around him.

Even if she felt safe around him. Her head was confused, she was distracted and not the way she wished to be distracted.

Alexis groaned and put her head down on the table. “Ready to train?” Caleb’s voice seemed deeper than usual, almost as if he had put something disgusting in his mouth. Alexis looked at him, he didn’t smile, and in fact his face looked like he was scowling. Alexis nodded her head and picked her body up from the computer seat; not before shutting everything down of course.

Something wasn’t quite right with Caleb this evening – as much as she hated to admit it. She knew when something was up with him – he had been living with her for around three nearly four weeks now. Alexis had grown accustomed to his moods; but this seemed different. Alexis stripped off her jumper before she even entered the room and dumped it down by the door. She didn’t carry anything else; she had left it all in the study where she had come straight from school.

Vladimir had spoken to her on the passing but as she had seemed distracted he had left her too her work – Louie hadn’t appeared yet. He was still sleeping away although she had expected him to wake before Caleb. That didn’t seem to be the case. “What are we doing Caleb?” She inquired titling her head and stopping just before the matts to wonder what he had planned for the day.

He didn’t turn to face her; instead he busied himself to push the matts together, as if they weren’t quiet perfect. “As far as training you in here is concerned we can’t do much else, I am sure Louie well help with some surprise attacks to get that side covered. It’s just your fitness I would say needs…improvements” Caleb had turned to look at her as he said the last word, the way his eyes scanning over her made her feel uncomfortable. He wasn’t looking at her the way he usually did, he was looking at her as the vampire, as the predator, as if she was his prey.

Alexis didn’t like it.

She felt like squirming under her gaze, her lips pouted slightly as his words sunk in – she had always thought of herself as quiet fit. She had never been one for too much exercise but with Louie running about the house and the size of her house, she often wondered how she could do more exercising than that.

With her last year of school; she wasn't required to take physical education either. So maybe Caleb was right in a sense. "Like how?" she pursed her lips in wonder and his lips quirked into a smirk on one side.

It looked evil. He swaggered closer towards her. "Laps, Jumps, Balance Beam, push ups, sit ups etc" his shoulders shrugged as if he didn't need to explain anything more, a shiver ran down her spine with his words, they were harsh, uncaring and not the usual words Caleb would use. Normally he explained everything to her, he let her know everything he planned to do – he let her come to grips with what they were going to learn before then teaching her. He was a good teacher and she had learned a lot from him, when he was his usual self anyway – this side of him, she doubted she would learn anything. This wasn't her normal teacher, *what had happened to him? Had she missed something?* She felt like something had happened while she was away – but it couldn't be possible, they had just woken up by the time she had come up.

Vladimir was still yawing and Louie was still sleeping, Caleb had been getting dressed according to Vladimir. *So why was he acting like this?* Opening and closing her mouth a few times she felt the urge to question him on it before shaking her head knowing it wouldn't do her any good. He was stubborn and he had something on his mind that he needed to work out.

"Where do I –" She started and was interrupted by his words "Start?" A small chuckle echoed roughly out of his lips, before he took a few steps backwards opening up his arms to indicate the room around him. "Start running. The room is big, run around the edges." He looked at her waiting for her to start, Alexis was used to listening to him and doing what he said but something felt different this time.

If he was going to be stubborn then why shouldn't she? She folded her arms in front of her chest and he raised an eyebrow and smirked. "For how many laps?" She inquired pursing her lips and holding back her contempt. His speed was fast, she had never seen him use it near her before, or not like this – not when he was acting *different*. He was inches away from her face within milliseconds of the words leaving her mouth, his arrogant smirk made Alexis's fingers twitch to slap him.

Not a reaction she wanted to use and one –at this point- she was sure he could stop. "Until I say stop" his words were harsh and his breath was warm against her face but it didn't give her any comfort. Frowning towards him she turned her back on him and jogged to the side of the room, giving him one last look before she started running around the room, first at a jogging pace for a few laps. She realised after the fifth lap that she was unfit – her legs began to burn, specifically her thighs. Her breathing was hard, laboured and Caleb stood in the middle of the room still watching her go around him countless numbers of times. He never turned or gave any other acknowledgement.

Alexis felt like questioning him. *Why was he doing this? What was he doing?* She was beginning to get ragged, her chest felt tight. She couldn't go on much longer. Alexis needed to tell him that, before she got the chance to, he was in front of her and she had to stop quickly. When her feet stopped she swung back slightly so she wouldn't hit him or become unbalanced. "Good.

Now do some sit ups" He pointed towards the matts in the middle.

Alexis didn't bother questioning him again she just moved to the middle and lay herself on the ground, after a moment she started to pull into a sit up. Caleb stood over her watching her intently and curiously. It wasn't something that Alexis was enjoying. She stared up towards the ceiling trying to get her gaze away from the strange vampire in front of her. *What was he up to?* "It's hard to concentrate with you watching over me all the time" Alexis stopped to finally look at Caleb.

"You're too easily distracted." Caleb pointed out his head tilted to the side. "And your acting like a Jerk" Alexis pouted slightly in which Caleb kneeled down towards and got to her level. His eyes level with hers.

They were mostly black, *what was happening to him?* "What is wrong with you?" Alexis leaned forward onto her knees to look at him. His smirk was half playful, half mischievous – much like the first night they had met. Alexis wanted to shrink back but instead she remembered Louie's words. You couldn't show a vampire fear. *You couldn't let them know you were scared. It would only excite them more.* Alexis kept facing him. She watched him to see his reaction and he leaned a little bit closer. "I'm working you" His statement was bland and held some weird statement behind it making Alexis's eyebrows knit together on the top of her head. "You wanted a teacher, not someone who would pet you" Caleb continued on although the smirk on his face was contradicting his words.

It was dangerous. "You've been teaching me before, this? Is different" Alexis pointed out. It was different especially to her. Normally they would joke, sometimes he would ignore her and that was normally the two Caleb's she had to deal with. This wasn't either of those two which made Alexis more curious as to why he was acting like this. "You're being an ass again" Alexis pointed out narrowing her eyes slightly. "Ah pup..." Caleb stood up; looking down on Alexis when he used the word pup she couldn't help but wince slightly. "You don't know how much of an ass I can be"

It may have been a part of who she was but it wasn't what she wanted to be. Alexis shook her head. "I'm leaving" She stood up and headed towards the door. "Have it on you wolfie. Come back when you're ready to learn something" Caleb answered moving over to where he had dumped some of his things.

Alexis had been looking for a distraction and instead she had to deal with a moody Caleb. She supposed one good point about it was, she had been distracted. She hadn't thought about Nicolas or his words during the full practice. But now she felt like she had too problems.

Caleb *and* Nicolas.

Caleb was acting strange and Nicolas well- Nicolas was a werewolf who seemed to think they shared some sort of connection. How could Alexis get rid of that idea? Was there such a way? Alexis found herself storming down the corridors and into the lounge where Louie sat. "Ah princess, what gives me this honour?" Louie's words rang out in a sing song voice. He was smiling bright and his body was tipped over the couch.

Alexis stormed into the room and sat down on the seat across from him. She folded her arms in front of her chest causing Louie to sit up with his eyebrows raised. “Is Mr. Fangs being too much for you?” Louie questioned seriously this time. Alexis nodded her head towards him. “He’s being an ass” Alexis pronounced out rather childishly, she regretted it as soon as she said it.

Caleb may have been acting like an ass but Alexis was acting like a child telling on him. She shook her head and slouched into her seat. “It doesn’t matter.” Alexis said after a moment, Louie stood to his feet and moved over towards her siting on the edge of her chair. “Mon Cherie, don’t worry about him. He’ll be gone in no time and we can go back to the way the three of us always were. I heard Vladimir has work in France next which means I can show you were I came from” Louie threw his arm over the chair behind her and leaned against it with his body.

Alexis looked up towards him and nodded her head. It made her sad to think that Caleb was leaving; she already couldn’t imagine her life without him. But at the same time maybe it was for the best. Caleb was bipolar at the best of times and with him here she seemed to be spending less time with Vladimir and Louie as if he intentionally kept them away.

Strange she couldn't help but think. Alexis head nodded but she didn't speak. "Now how is school, Vlad said you are enjoying it. You must be the smartest in the class. All those stupid humans have nothing on you" Louie charm had no bounds and Alexis couldn't help but smile and groan slightly. "Louieee" she shook her head and laughed slightly.

"There's no need to over exaggerate" she tilted her head towards him and he slipped into the single chair beside her. He pulled her into a tight hug. "I missed you, girly" Louie drawled out in his French accent causing Alexis to laugh and push at him. Louie was always over bearing. She manoeuvred herself out of the seat and turned to face him. "Thanks Louie. I'm going to catch up on my homework but thanks for cheering me up" Alexis smiled towards him as she turned to leave. "Not a problem, Cherie" Louie's voice followed her although she knew he hadn't moved.

As she exited into the corridor she automatically got the feeling of someone's eyes on her and she slowed her steps down before turning around. "Caleb" her hand came to her chest in relief when she saw Caleb leaning against the wall on the opposite side of the room she had just exited. "You scared me" She admitted, not thinking twice about it.

It was funny how sometimes she followed Louie's warnings and other times she didn't even think about them. "I am sorry" Caleb spoke surprising Alexis. Alexis was about to say it was alright, that it didn't matter but when he spoke he sounded sincere and it made Alexis wonder if he was actually talk about scaring her or about their earlier situation. "Sorry for my actions earlier. I don't know why I acted that way" Caleb shook his head and lowered it towards the floor.

Curiously Alexis watched him, *had he not done it on purpose? Had something set him off? Or was he just lying to her?*

Alexis wasn't sure which one to believe or where to even start questioning him. "It's okay" Alexis admitted waving her hands as if it were nothing, although she didn't know if she could forgive him so easily. "I need to go get some homework done." Alexis pointed towards the study in where she had done her homework lately.

Caleb was confusing and right now she didn't want to deal with him. She didn't want to deal with any of the current problems. She just wanted to dig into her work and finish it already. He nodded his head towards her although didn't answer. His eyes watched her as she turned to leave and Alexis made her way into the little room, where she had dumped her bag earlier. Her routine never changed. She was glad she had come up with this plan.

It made things so much easier for her. Sinking down into her chair she let out a deep sigh before focusing on her work. It was the best source of distraction.

20

Anti-wolf

"I just have the best idea!" Cassie's words were loud and Alexis hadn't even noticed her come into Home Room, she had been rather oblivious lately; focusing too much in her own head than on her own surroundings.

That seemed better though.

With Sandy and Marie sitting not that far away, Sandy always glaring at her or putting her in awkward situations for reasons she was sure *now* had something to do with Nicolas. Alexis never wanted anything to do with it though and she wished both of them would just leave her out of their relationship. She was finding it difficult enough to deal with werewolves in the school and vampire moods at home, plus she was sure something was up with Louie. She had hardly seen him in so long and that wasn't like Louie at all.

Vladimir would often meet her from school or he would see her before she went to her bed – not as much as she was used to sure but still it was more than what she had currently been seeing him. But there was enough confusion going on in her life without adding more problems too it. So she would have much preferred if Sandy and Nicolas could just back off, although that didn't seem to be happening anytime soon.

With a deep breath her eyes adjusted back to their surroundings and she smiled towards Cassie. "What's that?" Ashley and Katie had stopped their conversation and now stared at Cassie waiting to see what she had in store now. Chris and Jack hadn't even joined the conversation; they were talking to other boys not far away from the table they currently sat at. Cassie was beaming, her hair was wilder than usual, and it wasn't tied up or pulled back, instead it was all let loose which was very unlike Cassie. "Let's go shopping this Friday, we have formal coming up and a few birthday parties….." she waggled her eyebrows and Alexis could almost tell that Cassie was talking about her own birthday. "…So we need a few dresses and other outfits for them so it would be good for us to get an early start and at least scope out the new material…There are a lot of shops around here which we can show you, Alexis easily" Cassie smiled and Katie and Ashley nodded their head in agreement with her.

"Oh definitely, I need a new pair of Jeans as well, these ones are starting to ware and itch." Ashley chimed in touching her jeans as if to show off what she was talking about. "I need shoes as well" Katie pointed out and both Cassie and Ashely laughed "You always need shoes" Cassie added.

Katie folded her arms; sitting back in her chair she pretended to pout although couldn't really remove the smile from her face. "So what do you think Alexis? I could pick you up and we can head over to the shopping centre and we can see what we need to pick up from there" Cassie had turned around to look at

Alexis and her head tilted to the side waiting for an answer. Hoping for a yes.

Alexis bit her lip, her eyes searching over the girls in front of her who looked generally excited to be going on a shopping trip and Cassie was looking at her as if she wanted Alexis to come along. There was only one problem.

Vladimir. It hadn't been that difficult for her to come to school; but somehow she thought that with Caleb around she was going to have more trouble trying to get to go off herself. Friday was normally her stay in and study day. Cassie seemed to take her silence as a no and began rambling "..Now before you say no, you don't need to spend any money you can just have a look and if you see anything you can always pick it up later – your parents have got to agree to that right?" Cassie pursed her lips as if hoping to that it would persuade her. "Besides it will only be a couple of hours. You're not grounded or anything are you?" Ashely asked picking up a biscuit she had in her bag and taking a bite out of it, she leaned on the table focusing more on the biscuit than on Alexis or anyone else at the table. Alexis shook her head and smiled slightly at their question.

Grounded wasn't the word for what Alexis was.

Trapped wasn't one either, she was kept quiet close at hand for many reasons. She was a werewolf and she didn't want to be, she lived with vampires. Her life wasn't normal. "I'm not grounded but I will ask. I'll get back to you tomorrow?" Alexis nodded her head hoping she was convincing more towards herself than towards her new friends. After all she was going to be the one trying to talk to Vladimir about it.

With a deep breath she nodded her head. "Amazing" Cassie smiled at her in agreement. "So Ash what's your dress code going to be like? I was like flats and skirt" She turned her attention away from Alexis and they started to discuss what they would wear although Alexis was drifting away from the conversation and focusing on her thoughts. "I was going for a sundress" was the last thing she heard from Katie before it was all more like a blur in her ears.

They were talking but she couldn't quiet hear what about. She was trying to get the wording in her head right, she was going over how she was even going to ask Vladimir the question without Louie or Caleb being there. They would only make it more difficult to even say anything. She bit her lip and pushed her hands under her chin in order to balance her head and think a little bit better.

A habit she had never really grown out of over the years. She could always say it was for books, *that they need books for a certain class.* She pursed her lips considering if that idea would work; she never liked lying to Vladimir and she was sure that he would work it out when she didn't come home with any books but yet come home with clothes.

Another sigh left her lips when she realised the best thing to do was to tell him the truth and just hope for a good reaction. The bell rang loud in her ears pulling her out of her thoughts. Cassie, Ashley and Katie were still talking about clothes and what they would wear but now Chris and Jack had joined them – Chris had his arms around Cassie. They had all stood up to leave the class, slightly behind them Alexis grabbed her bag at her feet and moved to follow them out. Although with the mob of people leaving the room she couldn't quite get beside them. Her next class was with Cassie so there was no doubt she would catch up with her in no time. Relaxing she felt her shoulders drop and she shuffled out the class behind her peers.

The rest of the day was a slow blur; Cassie talked to her about the shopping trip, tempting her to go in American History 1. Alexis tried not to give her an answer either way, at least not until she could get home and talk to Vladimir. It amazed Alexis how Cassie could talk through the full class yet still always pass things. Alexis always listened and tried to write as much down as possible in class even while Cassie spoke to her – which she had learned was increasingly difficult after her last class where she had in fact written down what Cassie was saying during one of the classes.

Lucky for Alexis she had all the books she needed in Vladimir's Library. He had either looked them out for her starting school or had bought them. Not that Vladimir needed to buy many books he had collected a lot over the years he had been alive. Katie, Ashley and even Chris joined in talking to her at lunch to try and talk her into this shopping trip and how good it would be. Ashley teased both Jack and Chris about not attending because they didn't look good in dresses which Alexis had learned with human's sarcasm was always present and they liked to joke around.

Hearing the way they acted towards each other at the beginning Alexis had been shocked and embarrassed by the way they talked – now she had learned that it was how they did things. Alexis had grown use to it and had started to insert comments when she could, although she never felt confident insulting any of them.

She didn't know if she ever would. She ignored Nicolas's stares when he past her and even his attempts to talk to her when she was alone, which with Cassie was almost never. Luckily for her. She didn't know how to deal with him right now. She wanted him to get over her being his *mate* and perhaps move on to someone else.

Which Alexis could only think would happen if she started ignoring him, perhaps stayed away from him and showed him that she didn't want to date any werewolves. She didn't even want to be near werewolves right now. Although he didn't seem to live up to what Vladimir had built them up to be. She had seen Alex, Marie and Sandy at work and all of them lived up to Vladimir's words.

One out of four definitely wasn't going to change her views. By the time Alexis had gotten home, she had thought long and hard about what she was going to say to Vladimir and listening out, it sounded like no one was awake with a smile on her face, she dropped her bag off in her room before heading towards Vladimir's office.

Knowing if he was going to be anywhere at this time it would be there. Just like she thought, Vladimir was writing on his desk, with no Louie or Caleb to be seen. She chapped on his door lightly and his head bounced up, his eyes staring towards her before realising she wanted to speak to him. He sat up straight and pushed his pen on the desk before folding his hands in front of him. "Alexis, What can I do for you?" Alexis held still for a moment before moving into the room and shutting the door behind her. She knew how good the vampire's ears were in this house and Vladimir's room was good for masking sounds. She had learned that when Vladimir had locked Louie in it once for misbehaving – although Vladimir had never explained how he had misbehaved towards Alexis. She knew that it worked in her favour right now.

After shutting the door she moved to sit in the chair across from Vladimir, he had raised his eyebrows and a small smile had crossed his lips at her actions. "Something that you wish our guest not to hear?" he inquired and Alexis couldn't help but echo his smile. He obviously found what she was doing amusing and perhaps liked that fact she had come to him about something.

Alexis felt guilty considering she hadn't really come for the reason he would more than likely want. "It's nothing like that. I wanted to ask you a question although I didn't want Louie or Caleb to interrupt. Although by the time I think they are still sleeping" Alexis checked her watch and was sure this was normally when they would still be in her bed. Vladimir sat back in his chair offering her the opportunity to continue.

Which after looking towards her feet Alexis did. "Some of the girls at school wanted to go shopping for a party that is coming up at school and I was asked to go with them. So I'm here to ask if I can?" Alexis looked towards Vladimir after she spoke, to assess his reaction. "..go that is?" She added in after a second thought thinking because of his silence she hadn't been too clear. But then again he normally always used the silence to think; and Alexis was speaking mostly because she was nervous and wasn't sure what else to do. Vladimir's head was nodding before he spoke and Alexis's mouth opened and closed a few times sure that maybe he was discussing something in his head. "Yes of course, when?" Vladimir watched her curiously and Alexis couldn't help but smile slightly. She had misjudged him. He had said yes.

"Friday?" She questioned not quite sure if he had completely decided on it yet and not wanting to say anything to change his mind. "Very well. I assume you will need money to attend; I have a card already in your name. I shall give it to you on Friday for you to go" Very confused and excited, Alexis nodded her head not knowing what else to say. *He had a card for her? A money card? A card with money on it.* Alexis had expected many answers and she had gone through many situations in her head although this hadn't been one of them.

Most of them ending on her telling her new *human* friends that she had too much work to get through or that she really didn't want to go shopping; maybe next time. There had been very few – if any- where she could go back and tell them yes. "Thank you?" She was still trying to piece everything together and that was why it came out more like a question rather than a statement. Vladimir smiled slightly, his lips hooking at the corners.

He didn't say anything else, he merely watched her. She nodded her head as if confirming her thank you, as she stood to her feet. She hesitated a few times as if she was looking to say something else, or have him say something else. But they didn't, so she left. Trailing back to her room she changed into her PJ's and started to study.

Before she knew it, she was sleeping, the stress of worrying about the situation had gotten to her and she slept right through to the next morning. When she got up; she cursed straight away looking at the time; she had missed training with Caleb. More than likely he had come into her room and tried to wake her with no luck. She had been shattered for more reasons than she physically knew. She'd need to catch up with him later; they would be heading to their bed. Getting up she went through her morning process of getting ready before heading out to the car like she always did.

"You can come! That's great to hear" Cassie's words echoed through her ears as the girl squeaked out her response. She had pulled Alexis in to a tight hug. Alexis smiled and hugged the girl back awkwardly before Cassie was pushing at her shoulders to look at her face, the smile beamed on her face. "I can't believe it. Ep! We are actually going to go shopping. I have to go find

Ash right now. She bet that you wouldn't be able to come and I so have to rub this in her face…." Alexis stumbled over her words, did they really think that much of her.

Ash had thought she wouldn't come. That kind of made her feel sad, but Cassie's smile never faded and she couldn't put a downer on the girl's extensive mood. Alexis nodded her head and Cassie pulled her into another hug before running away down the hall in search for her friend. Alexis smiled and shook her head, unable to understand what was going on in that girl's head in those moments but she couldn't help but smile.

Turning around she lowered her head and began to walk forward, her head in her thoughts. Sandy in front of her.

Wait! What?

Her eyes shot up and she half wondered how it had come to her head like that. She hadn't been watching where she was going but yet somehow she knew Sandy was standing in front of her. Looking up she saw exactly that. Sandy didn't look happy. She didn't look in a good mood and somehow Alexis knew it was directed towards her. Alexis looked for a direction to go but knew she wouldn't get far. She looked around for someone that could save her from this confrontation but Cassie had disappeared and the corridor was emptying.

"Sandy" She tried to offer a smile although it didn't make it to her face. She knew the only way to get out of this was to agree with the wolf and to smile along like nothing was happening. She didn't know what Sandy wanted and Alexis didn't really care about her problems especially if they had anything to do with werewolves. Alexis did know that what Louie said about vampires also applied to werewolves. You couldn't show your fear, unlike vampires though Alexis had a deeper fear of werewolves.

Mostly because she was supposed to be one herself. "You need to back off" Sandy hissed through her teeth and Alexis felt confused. "Okay? I can do that just tell me what from and it's done" Alexis held up her hands as if trying to calm Sandy down. Sandy's eyes flashed with anger, she was frustrated, annoyed and she looked scary. "Nicolas" Sandy growled, her hands pushed on her hips and Alexis's heart sunk. Now this was going to be more difficult than she expected. "Ehm..I don't know how that would work" Alexis admitted feeling rather nervous. "I would love nothing more to stay away from all of you guys but you guys keep seeking me out. That makes it rather difficult for me" Alexis admitted biting her lower lip and wondering if perhaps Sandy had another plan to keep her away from these wolves.

Although she highly doubted it. "I don't care! Stay away from him. Leave the school. Stay with Cassie all the time. That is not my concern but Nicolas is, so stay away from him" Sandy grounded out and Alexis was sure the girl was about to explode. *Great Advice,* Alexis had to resist the urge to roll her eyes. Her eyes flashed and they looked like those of a wolf which made Alexis step back. She didn't mind facing up to these wolves while they were humans but as wolves she stood no chance. "You have no idea how much I will try" Alexis muttered under her breath and Sandy ignored her words, she was breathing heavily. She wouldn't change in the school though would she? Alexis didn't know. In these moments anything could happen.

Alexis nodded a little. "He is mine!" Sandy's growl vibrated through her chest and she took a step closer to Alexis causing Alexis to gulp. Her knees were shaking and she was sure she felt like they were about to give way. Obviously the wolf had some issues and Alexis wasn't the one she needed to be talking to.

"I get it! He's yours" Alexis felt like the words were dragged out her mouth. She didn't want to say them even though she knew they would calm Sandy. Nicolas was the one that thought she was his mate. Sandy needed to talk to Nicolas. Alexis didn't want to get in the middle of their relationship and although she felt some attraction towards him, it wasn't enough to risk her life and stand in front of Sandy. She would rather have stayed away from all the wolves. It would make things so much easier. Alexis nodded her head although she was unsure of how she could keep that promise.

With that Sandy growled once more before pushing past Alexis. Her shoulder bashed against Alexis's and Sandy stormed down the hall way without looking back. Alexis's eyes followed her, when she couldn't see Sandy anymore she sighed deeply and shook her head and walked towards her class. “Sucks to be me” Alexis mumbled.

21

Show me

Alexis pace quickened, her footsteps echoed in her ears and her heart rate was beginning to pick up. *He* was following her yet again. She had been ignoring each of his attempts at talking to her again, just like Sandy had warned her but even ignoring him wasn't working.

He still searched her out and followed her around. She hadn't seen much of the other werewolves at least since then. But he was still being a pain. Between Nicolas's stalking and Caleb's mood swings she wasn't sure which was worse, they were both giving her a complex. The two were as bad as each other. She didn't know how to handle either of them. Her frustration with him was growing and she knew that Sandy would make good on her threat. She wasn't going to take the threat lightly but Nicolas was testing her now.

Alexis's lips moved into a straight line as she turned around to face him. "Will you stop following me!" Nicolas seemed surprised by her outburst but at the same time the smile he held was obvious that he was pleased with her acknowledgement of him. Alexis grunted under her breath, lunch time always left the corridors empty.

They were beginning to empty fast, Alexis's eyes scanned around. "Just come with me" Nicolas reached for her hand and began to tug her down the corridors towards the outside of the school. Alexis had visions of him pulling her towards other wolves and she pulled her hand out of his. "Where?" She questioned stopping her footsteps and causing Nicolas to turn around. "Just outside of school grounds. I promise it will just be us. No other werewolves." Nicolas answered as if he had heard her thoughts and she eyed him suspiciously.

He always seemed to know what made her nervous and what she was thinking, it was as if she was in her thoughts. "I don't think that is a good idea" Alexis answered her voice wavering slightly as she thought about Sandy's threat; it was only a few days ago that it had happened and the words still echoed in her head.

Nicolas seemed to find her amusing in this, he shook his head. "I think it's a great idea. Please just give me lunch today" Nicolas pleaded with her, his deep brown eyes watching her and trying to make her agree to what he was saying. He wasn't using any of his alpha power, although he doubted that it would work on a Lupei. Alexis pursed her lips and scanned around making sure Sandy wasn't anywhere to be seen. She didn't want to be stuck here with him, and she didn't want to be stuck here with any werewolves but at the same time – if she could get them off her back in any way shape or form then she had to try it. "Just lunch today?" she queered and Nicolas smiled triumphantly as he nodded his head. He hadn't thought she would even give him that.

Alexis nodded her head and Nicolas held out his hand towards her. Alexis looked at him for a moment. *Should she really risk being seen holding his hand?* There was a silent pull in her that wanted to reach out and take his hand. There was always a pull in her that wanted to be close to him and she had ignored it this much. She had to keep ignoring it. She looked away from him, Nicolas didn't push anymore he merely turned around and digging his hands into his pockets he offered her to walk beside him with the tilt of his head.

Alexis fell into step beside him and they both walked out of the school, Nicolas led them behind the school and towards the back gates. Alexis looked at him curiously although he didn't offer anything more than a smile. Alexis stopped at the gates as Nicolas manoeuvred one of the gates out of the way so that there was a small space for them to fit through. He waved his hand; Alexis hesitated for a moment before bending and going through the small amount of space.

At the other side she waited for Nicolas to come through before questioning him. "What are we doing out here?" her voice held all her anxiety and fear, of where they were going. Nicolas actually looked hurt; he didn't understand why she couldn't trust him.

Well part of him did. Part of him knew that something had happened in her life that had made her scared of werewolves and although he couldn't openly ask her what that was he knew that he had to figure it out. With a deep sigh he walked past her, moving into the wooded area a little bit more. "Just somewhere we can talk a little better." He answered and although she hesitated again she still followed after him without a word. *Why was she following him in the first place? Why had she agreed to this?* She should have at least stayed on school grounds.

Alexis rolled her eyes at her thoughts. *It was too late now.* Something inside of her knew that and she knew she might as well continue what was going on right now. She stopped only when Nicolas stopped in front of her. He turned to face her. "I'm a little bit of a different type of wolf than you" Nicolas admitted and Alexis's eyes squinted at him curiously. There were different *types* of werewolves. She didn't know if that made her more scared or less. She swallowed the growing lump in her throat deciding to ask some questions she had on her mind, she knew she wasn't going to get another chance.

"What type of werewolf are you?" she questioned causing Nicolas's lips to turn up at the corners of his mouth. "Villalobos" Nicolas's words came out and Alexis understood them straight away. Spanish was a language she knew although not much of it, she had been starting to learn it. Villalobos was a word she understood. "Town of wolves?" Alexis said surprising Nicolas. His head bounced into a nod "Not many people know that translation. The only reason I know it is because I'm the next alpha and we get taught some history of the pack" Nicolas admitted and Alexis half wondered why.

Alexis nodded not knowing what to say to that. "How many breeds of werewolves are there?" Alexis half wondered about all the werewolves and if they were all the same. *What ones did Vladimir say was bad? Did he mean all of them? Or was it specific ones?*

She wanted to question him on it but knew questioning him would only end in more questions for her. She had to find a way to get more information perhaps through Caleb but then again that all depended on his mood. “There used to be 6, but one has dwindled and we thought was instinct” Nicolas answered and Alexis wondered what he meant by that, her head turned away. She didn’t want to be curious about werewolves; she didn’t want to know anything about them.

Alexis shook her head of all the questions stuck in her mind. She wouldn’t ask them. She needed a change in topic perhaps one in which would scare him away from her. Keep him at arm’s length from her. “You need to stay away from me” Alexis told him, she didn’t lift her head to see his reaction neither did she need to. His intake of breath and quickening heartbeat said enough that he wasn’t going to agree to this. “Why?” he questioned half-heartedly, as if he didn’t much care about the answer to the question.

Alexis shook her head debating on what to tell him, she couldn’t very well just open out the truth with him. Shee would just get Sandy into trouble, which in return would end bad for Alexis – no matter how much Nicolas tried to protect her. He never seemed to be there when Sandy was. Sandy was sly and cunning and when she saw something she wanted she went for it and apparently she wanted Nicolas.

Although Alexis disliked that thought she knew it was for the best. Not only was Nicolas a werewolf but he was an alpha. That just made things worse. She knew what that meant well enough to know Nicolas was at the top of the chain and Sandy was no doubt up there as well.

Alexis couldn't deal with some competitive wolves; she didn't even like the idea of dealing with wolves in the first place. "I won't be staying here long. You're pack is in enough turmoil here without bringing me into the picture for the little while I am here. I don't change into a wolf. I don't want to sit and talk around the table with you guys. I just want to go to school for my last year" Alexis let out a deep breath as she said the words; they were the truth after all. She didn't want to be dragged into all of this nonsense with the wolves. She just wanted to get on with her school work and perhaps even go shopping with Cassie and get some *human* experience before she was trapped back up in a house with Louie and Vladimir again.

She was Immortal and that wasn't normal for a wolf – Vladimir had explained that much too her. Alexis didn't see the point in getting caught up in mortal werewolves. She didn't see the point in getting caught up in werewolves if she were honest. "We're not as bad as you think, Lex. We're not dangerous, just misunderstood. I mean there are five werewolves in this school before you came and no one has been hurt. No one has turned into a werewolf randomly. There have been no '*anima*l' deaths around here suspected of being werewolves in a long time" Nicolas tried soothing her, he took a step towards her and she matched it by taking one backwards.

Nicolas stopped and his hands dropped lazily beside him. "I could never understand what you've been through. I couldn't begin to understand what you're going through right now but I can assure you it will never happen again. None of my pack will ever hurt you" Alexis wanted to laugh, he could speak for himself but he could not speak for his pack, not when she had already been threatened by a member of them. Alexis head turned away, she gritted her teeth. She couldn't just sit back and watch all of this happen in front of her.

She wanted out. Now.

"Try telling your pack members that first. You may feel that way but I know they do not. After all I have already been threatened by one of them" Surprised, Nicolas watched her before cursing under his breath. "Sandy" Alexis felt an awkward smile on her face; of course he would know who it was. Nicolas didn't even have to think about it. "She's….I….Sandy won't hurt you" Nicolas couldn't find the right words to say to her but eventually settled on Sandy wouldn't hurt her.

Alexis almost wanted to trust him with it. She almost wanted to believe him. "I think you should tell her that not me. She's pretty adamant that I am stepping on her toes here" Alexis wasn't sure why her body was over heated talking about this. It wasn't as if she felt passionate about this matter she was merely stating a fact.

Looking away from Nicolas she tried to give herself time to think over what she was saying and calm her heart rate down again. Living with vampires all this time did tend to have its advantages – one of which was being able to listen and slow down your heart rate. "With Sandy I am obviously not safe" Alexis ended on a sigh; her fist went from being clenched to hanging by her side. She didn't want to fight, not with Nicolas nor with Sandy. She enjoyed learning to fight; it burnt off her unused energy which would have probably made her turn into a werewolf, and it gave her something else to think about, it gave her a reprieve from thinking about the scratching in her mind.

Not that she had ever admitted that to Louie, Vladimir or Caleb. They didn't need to know that reason; it wouldn't change anything after all. Nicolas's sigh was one of defeat as if he had been wishing it wouldn't have to come to this. He didn't want to have to explain his relationship with Sandy. "She's jealous" Nicolas finally said perking up Alexis ears and finally making her stare at him. His face was blushed slightly, he body seemed defeated, and his eyes looked to the ground as he spoke.

They had switched positions and now Alexis found herself staring at him. Her green eyes skimming over his movements and watching his reactions to what he was saying. He seemed so young at times – like right now. "She doesn't want to accept the fact that I ended it with her and she is taking it out on you. We had been dating for about half a year or there abouts, my father hadn't exactly agreed to it. He called it a fancy fling with a wolf until I found my mate. I thought it was more than that, so did she. When I found out it wasn't, she didn't take it well and because I won't let her near me again she's taking it out on you because I care about you" Nicolas didn't want to look up, he didn't want to see her reaction to what he had just said. His ears had red tips and Alexis couldn't help but find that cute. Alexis found the situation to intense, she wanted to hug him, she wanted to comfort him but at the same time she knew his decision had been because of her arrival.

He had made this decision because he thought she was his mate. So technically that made it Alexis's fault; Sandy had every right to blame her. Nicolas again sighed and Alexis couldn't find the urge to look at him. She stared to the left and towards the ground.

Why did she have the urge to ask all these questions about werewolves now? She didn't want to know about her species. She didn't even want to be a part of it. Whether Vladimir was talking about all werewolves of just one out of the six that Nicolas was talking about, she didn't care. She just wanted to get through school and then both Caleb and Nicolas would leave and she would end up in France with Louie and Vladimir. She had to keep looking to that point, not matter how much her heart ached to think about it.

It was the better option. She didn't want to leave Nicolas but neither did she want to leave Caleb. She couldn't live with both after all one was a vampire and the other was a werewolf. The only reason she had both of them right now was because neither of them knew about each other. Something wet touched her hand causing her to flinch and her eyes to snap towards it.

It was a wolf!

Alexis moved fast, stepping backwards she found herself falling backwards. That didn't stop her as the wolf approached her, she scrambled backwards. Her hands dragged her through the dirt, it was dried and the weeds cut her hands as she backed away.

The wolf stopped in front of her sitting down on its back end. Alexis couldn't stop; she kept going backwards until her back hut the tree. She looked up and she saw the branches extended above her head. But her eyes couldn't stay there for long, they snapped back down towards the wolf. Her eyes tried to scan behind him, *where was Nico?* The wolf in front of her was looking at her, its head tilted to the side and his black eyes watching her actions. Its brown coat was thick and ruffled it lay down in front of her causing her to pull her feet in. Its face was just a little away from her and it whined low in its throat. *Was this Nicolas?* The oddest thought stuck in her head as she watched the wolf's actions. Her throat was dry; her hands were cut from the stones and weeds. She refused to look at them though; she refused to look away from the wolf. It's tongue stuck out his mouth and he panted.

"Nicolas?" Alexis inquired unsure if this was actually him in front of him. She wasn't sure if that would actually make her feel better if it was. The wolf let out a howl as if agreeing with her causing her to jump. He pushed himself forward towards her although kept low.

Alexis watched it nervously with wide eyes. This could not be happening right now. Human werewolves were hard enough to deal with and now she had to deal with one in its wolf form! This couldn't get much worse. The wolf moved closer until its paw was touching Alexis's feet. It's head nearly in her lap and he urged her to pet him by pushing its head towards her hands. Alexis was shaking, her hands were vibrating and her throat had dried up to the point she couldn't even voice what she wanted to say. She wanted to tell Nicolas to change back, to tell him to stop it.

He had to listen to her right? He had said he didn't want to hurt her. Alexis swallowed trying to clear the dryness in her throat although it wasn't working. Her hand shakily touched Nicolas, his fur wasn't as rough as she expected but then again it wasn't soft either. It had a weird texture towards it, almost in between both. She pulled her hand back as soon as he moved and in front of her the wolf began to mould into Nicolas once again.

Nicolas's normal brown eyes finally looked towards her causing her to relax slightly, he looked curious and anxious over her and his mouth opened to speak but the bell rang in the far distance causing both of their gazes to look at the school.

Lunch was over.

Nicolas stood up offering Alexis his hand and they both headed back onto the school grounds in silence. Nicolas didn't know what to say to her, he didn't know how to comfort her since he didn't know what the problem was. She was frozen in her position when he had been a wolf and any movement seemed to scare her as if she were a deer stuck in head lights. He had thought that showing her he was a wolf would have been easy, that she would have thought of him more like a dog that wanted to be petted and perhaps her wolf would have sensed his and came out.

But he had seen no signs of her wolf just like Sandy had said, she hadn't growled and her eyes had never shown much of anything. The only thing Alexis had done to show her wolf was to Marie and Sandy on her first day.

They were the only two to have seen anything. Nicolas just wanted to help her but he didn't know what to do. He didn't know she didn't want to be helped.

22

Grin and bear it

Her room was pitch black, the house was unseeingly quiet for a house full of vampires. Apart from the drumming in her ear, Alexis felt confused on that thought and found herself pushing up from her bed to follow the noise.

Vladimir was beside her, his face was deadly serious causing Alexis to sit up and rub her eyes. “Vlady? What’s up?” she questioned with a yawn causing her hand to cover her mouth at the end of the sentence. Vladimir never woke her in the middle of the night especially since she had been at school. In fact it had been years since she had been woken up at all.

Normally her half day – half night timetable had kept that from needing to happen but now that she was in a semi human timetable she guessed that had changed. “I need you to get up and get ready. You have a visitor” Vladimir’s voice was tight and unpleased by the situation. Alexis tried to think who would come and see her that Vladimir didn’t like.

The wolves pasted her mind for a moment but she knew that they wouldn’t be having this conversation if a wolf was in the house. Vladimir would have merely told the wolf to get lost, evicted Alexis from school and then they would move house which would have been how Alexis found out about the situation. She would be the last to know. It had to be a vampire.

An certain Elder perhaps. No other vampire was allowed to see her after all. She slid out of bed with a nod, causing her to yawn again, when she slipped on her sheets, Vladimir helped steady her. “Thanks” she mumbled moving towards her wardrobe to pull some clothes out. She didn’t think she had to look her best.

Half asleep she pulled her trousers over her shorts and a jumper on top of her PJ's t-shirt. She couldn't find the effort to get completely changed and when she turned back around Vladimir was watching her with curiosity. "I'm too tired to get ready for our guest. Does this suit?" She questioned since he didn't move towards the door straight away. Vladimir seemed to come out of his daze and he nodded his head before moving towards the door.

Alexis followed suit in her socks. She couldn't find the urge to grab shoes from the opposite side of her room so instead she walked out half sleeping. She stumbled down the hallway, following Vladimir's elegant movements; she was ushered into the main lounge. "Ah Alexandra, such a pleasant surprise. Sorry if we woke you, I know your timetable has changed recently from what it was when I used to visit" Daniel's voice was strong and it caused Alexis to peak behind Vladimir to see Daniel. She had not seen him in a few years, their chats had been frequent when she was a child and as she got older they became less and less.

Caleb was there in the room as well, sitting on the chair behind Daniel. Apart from that no one else was in the room. She couldn't look at Caleb though, he had upset her enough over the past little while and she had enough to deal with without acknowledging another situation, especially when she was so tried. Vladimir looked tense beside her as she rubbed her eyes once again trying to get the sleep out of them.

A yawn over took her again. "Sorry" She spoke with her hand over her mouth causing Daniel's mouth to pull up in a smirk. "You seem to be quiet tired. Have you been busy lately?" Daniel inquired with a satisfied smile; Alexis eyed both Caleb and Vladimir at this point. She hadn't been told what she was and wasn't allowed to say right now. But she guessed she should just tell him the truth.

If Vladimir hadn't wanted her to say anything then he would have told her in her room. He would have found a way. "With school, homework and training it has me worn out most days, especially during the week. I am a bit more awake at the weekend" Alexis admitted as again she covered her mouth for another yawn, the more she thought about it the more she felt like yawning.

Both Caleb and Vladimir were quiet beside them. Daniel's head tilted to the side. "You have been training?" Daniel inquired his eyes never leaving Alexis face; he always watched her reaction and his face always held its amused grin on it. He was completely dressed in a black suit, a white shirt underneath with a red tie.

Alexis found him handsome for an older man; he had an ageless quality about him especially his eyes. They told Alexis he was much older than most cared to admit. He had knowledge beyond years. "Caleb has been teaching me to defend myself and …keep up my fitness" Alexis found her breath hitching on her last few words, after all he had been rude to her and although he had been talking about her fitness; Alexis knew there was probably better ways to do it than what he had suggested. It could have been like every other lesson but instead of that he was acting like a jerk.

"Caleb?" Daniel finally looked away from her although he didn't turn to look at Caleb either, his eyes merely drifted to the side. "She's scared she'll meet a werewolf and not know how to defend herself against it" Caleb's voice was cold and uncaring and Alexis half wondered why he was even telling Daniel anything. Caleb's eyes were darker than usual although not completely black. He was casually sitting over a chair his back sat against one arm and his feet hung over the other side.

The room was lit by the fireplace although there was another source of light from the other side of the room. A tall looming lamp which seemed half awake. "Interesting. Werewolves are dangerous, I can understand why you would want to defend yourself but you must understand that the best way to defend yourself against one would be to change into one" Daniel spoke without much concern his hands echoed movements in front of him as he spoke.

Alexis looked down on his words not knowing how else to react. She couldn't change into a werewolf, she wouldn't. It wasn't her.

“Fascinating” Daniels voiced as he watched her, although he looked like he was holding back from saying something more. “And how are you? Are you enjoying staying here? Eating enough?” Daniel asked after a moment of silence, he changed the subject so easily. It was like he didn’t care in particular what answer he got as long as he got an answer.

Alexis wasn’t sure why he actually came around to see her. Her head nodded. “Of course” she answered much less enthusiastically as she used to answer him. She used to answer him with extra, as if a simple answer wasn’t enough, she had to explain to him what exactly was happening and when it had happened.

That seemed like such a long time ago now, to her it even seemed like she was a different person. “You’re not as talkative as you used to be, Alexandra. You use to tell me everything. A lot more than I needed to know but I enjoyed it” Daniel had moved closer to her now and she found her gaze looking up toward him, he wasn’t as tall as Vladimir or Caleb but he was taller than her. Maybe just under a head taller than her. Alexis didn't know what to say to him, she didn't know what the reason was for that fact but she supposed part of it was because of the wolves and the other part was because of Vladimir, Louie and Caleb.

They were her family – very dysfunctional family but one never the less. "As long as you are well little one I have no qualms" Daniel smiled down towards her. As quickly as he had said it, he had turned around towards Caleb. "What about you, Ambrogino?" *Latin:* Alexis was sure she recognised it, Vladimir had been called it once or twice before.

Alexis was sure it meant "*Little Immortal one"* Alexis didn't want to seem interested in this conversation between Daniel and Caleb – part of her wanted to leave, in fact she had hoped that Vladimir would step up but he did not. Vladimir in fact hadn't spoken once since leaving her room, he had to have orders not too. Daniel smirked casting a glance towards her before looking at Caleb. "It's constricting. Alia causa est ut veniret?" Caleb continued on in Latin, although Caleb spoke in a language Alexis couldn't understand she could identify it easily.

Alexis rolled her eyes and Daniel couldn't help but chuckle as his child changed the language, to one only the vampires in the room could understand. "Qui transit per. Curiosus is video in dorsum et Leonardus in hac Elizabeth. Ego sum....Kill two birds with one stone" Daniel changed back mid-sentence to speak to them. As he turned back around to face Alexis and Vladimir. "Me, et non creditis." Caleb murmured under his breath causing Daniel to smile back towards him. "No they do not trust you, not yet anyway" Daniel admitted in English back towards him although he didn't turn her around.

"And how are you enjoying Caleb being here?" Daniel inquired again in front of Alexis once again; she could feel her cheeks blushing at the statement. *How did she answer it?* She thought she had liked it but lately with his mood swings – who was she kidding Caleb always had mood swings right from the beginning. They were just becoming worse as of lately. "He's different from Vladimir and Louie. I think he's... bipolar" Alexis admitted nervously, her eyes glancing towards Vladimir.

Alexis had insulted Louie many a times and Vladimir had seemed amused by them but she didn't know how other vampires would take to insulting their *"child".* This caused Daniel to laugh rather dramatically, he held on to his sides and Vladimir's eyebrows lifted up as if he had never heard his sire laugh like this before.

Alexis's eyes cast away from Vladimir and back to the Elder vampire. "I have never heard Caleb be called Bipolar before; He has been cursed for many things but never that…" Daniel trailed off as he recovered from laughing to look at the young werewolf.

A smile creased on his face that Alexis could have mistaken for caring before he had turned again and was facing Caleb. "There must be parts of you I even don't know yet" Daniel talked to his child with a chuckle which caused Caleb to make a noise that was incomprehensible as he shrugged. "I think that's enough enjoyment for one night. I will take my leave and return in a few weeks. Sorry for waking you up little one. I hope you can get back to sleep tonight" Daniel had pulled a jacket on that had been draped over Caleb's chair and he moved towards Alexis, patting her on the head when he called her a little one. "It's nice to see you again, Vladimir. Please visit me sometime. I hear you wish to move to France next even though I suggested London. Whichever you decide I am sure it will be good for you" Daniel acknowledged Vladimir for the first time before leaving through the door.

Vladimir moved after him, asking him something Alexis could not quiet hear through the doors. She was still tired. Caleb titled his head back as Daniel left and closed his eyes. Alexis wasn't sure whether she wanted to leave the room or not.

Caleb hadn't looked at her this full meeting, although she had tried to avoid looking at him as well. He had talked about her as if she wasn't' there. Alexis wasn't happy about that but at the same time she didn't know how to react to it. She turned to leave but Caleb was at the door first. "Am I really that bad that you want to leave without saying anything to me?" Caleb questioned and Alexis tried to see his eyes through his hair to see whether he was being the nice Caleb or whether he was playing with her again.

She couldn't see his eyes; he had intentionally dipped his head in such a way so she couldn't see them. Sometimes these vampires annoyed her. "Only when you're an ass" Alexis answered back with her hands on her hips, she tried and failed to surpass the yawn that was coming on. "You're cute when you're tried. You pulled on clothes and you put your jumper back to front and you're hair is puffy" Caleb's smile was kind, although it caused Alexis to pull on her jumper trying to see if he was telling the truth. As she thought he was, the tag on her shirt suggested she had it on backwards, no wonder Vladimir had looked at her weirdly in her room. He must have been wondering if she knew her clothes were on backwards.

"Damn" Alexis cursed trying to pull the jumper off, once it was off she couldn't be bothered changing it, she was just going back to her bed after all where was the use on pulling it back on to walk along the half.

Caleb was watching her, his eyes darkened, his lips pulsed as if his fangs were threatening to break out causing Alexis to falter on what she was about to say. "Cal?" she questioned knowing that he would call her on the nickname only if he was the dark Caleb and he would laugh at it if he was the normal Caleb. Caleb seemed to turn away from her. Not a reaction to match either side that Alexis knew. "I'm fine. You better get back to your bed" Alexis wanted to question him, she wanted to ask about what was wrong, check if he was okay but she knew with his nature not to do that so instead she nodded her head and moved past him towards the hallway and back to her room to sleep.

23

Coincidence? I think not.

Friday came by quiet quickly after the commotion with Caleb, Daniel and Nicolas. With those three in her life she was lucky if anything would happen slowly again. Daniel's night visits were almost definitely going to be becoming more frequent and with Caleb switching between playing friends and ignoring her she was beginning to get whiplash and with his new mean personality she couldn't decide which was worse.

Then she had Nicolas at school, despite his words he followed her around like a lost puppy dog – even though she had told him about Sandy. He didn't seem to care very much.

Vladimir had agreed to let her go with the girls on the condition that his driver drops her off. So he had, he had dropped her off at the door and almost instantly Cassie had jumped on her as soon as she had got out of the car and she was being dragged about the mall.

"We have to start at stitches!" Cassie squealed pulling Alexis towards a store. "We always do what you want first, let's do Urban" Ash seemed determined to get what she wanted. Alexis felt at ends although she listened to what both girls were saying.

Katie added in words every now and again as if trying to stay out of the fight but both Cassie and Ash were determined to pull her in on it. Before long they had settled on a shop which was neither Urban nor Stitches. Alexis hadn't been able to see the name as she was dragged into it. "You need to try on this" Cassie pulled a dress out in front of Alexis to measure it against her as if judging what size she was, she switched sizes and then pushed Alexis towards the changing rooms. "Try it on and let us see what it looks like"

With a sigh Alexis found herself in a changing room, ever since she had turned up she was being pulled around and Cassie had squealed when Alexis had brought out the credit card saying she did have money to spend. Alexis pushed out of her jeans and her jumper; she pulled off her tank top folding them into a neat pile at the corner of the dressing room she fixed the dress into position before looking in the mirror.

The dress was baby blue in colour, it stopped just before her knees and had a darker blue belt going across the middle, and the circular neck line had an added layer of frills attached to it and the straps that held the dress to her shoulders were thin.

Alexis looked like a proper girl; she blushed slightly at the thought. She had never much been one for wearing dresses; it wasn't that she didn't want to wear them. She just couldn't find the occasion to wear them. "Are you ready?" She heard Cassie's voice which jolted her out of her thoughts; she smiled and opened the curtains to see Cassie smiling at her.

"Ready" Cassie beamed at her, and Ashley was beside her assessing the way she looked, beside her Katie was dressed in a long pink dress with her hair tied back in a bun. "You look great although the neckline doesn't look quite right. Let me get something else for you…" Ashley turned and disappeared for a moment. “That looks lovely on you, Katie” Alexis decided to turn her attention away from her own dresses and towards the other girl dressed up, Cassie did the same thing.

Pulling on her arms she made the girl twirl in front of her. “She’s right. That dress suits you perfectly. Is it for formal? I thought you wanted to stay away from pink this year?” Cassie asked without taking her eyes from her dress. “I debated it but when I saw this dress I just couldn’t help but try it on you know” Katie smoothed down the front of the dress with a small smile on her face.

Alexis watched her, her head tilted to the side. Katie seemed to be dreaming off in her own world and Alexis wondered what she was thinking of. “Why not try a yellow as well? Just to be sure. We can keep this one aside just in case” Cassie recommended, as Ashley came back passing another dress to Alexis. “Try this one” Alexis turned and headed back towards the dressing room stripping off the dress. “Let me take this one” Ashley’s hand came into the room and grabbed the other dress from Alexis.

Alexis had jumped out of the way, not thinking that anyone would come in while she was getting ready. "Yeah that is fine" Alexis caught her breath as the hand disappeared out of the room with the baby blue dress and Alexis began to pull the other one in. This one was also blue except it was more of a deep blue.

There were no straps, it just pulled against her chest and dipped over her chest in the right positions. The bottom of the dress was loose and when she moved it moved as well, the bodice was like a corset although didn't feel as tight as one. It was covered in jewels which slowly got less the further down you got. This dress went down to her thighs.

Alexis couldn't believe how good the dress looked on; Ashley knew exactly what she was talking about. When Alexis stepped out, Cassie gasped "That's your dress" She squealed slightly, Cassie was dressed in something else. She had a short black and silver dress on. The belt at her waist split up the dress. The bottom was all puffy and black and the top was like a tiger skin black and silver. It had a bow attached to the left side;

Cassie had never suited something more. Her messy lion's mane hair was pulled back in to a bun although some had got free and dangled down to her neck. "I could say the same for you..." Alexis admired Cassie, she had short legs but in that dress they looked longer. Cassie giggled and twirled around in her dress.

"Do you think? I wasn't so sure on the length. Normally my legs are too short to suit something like this" Cassie pushed the bottom of the dress down slightly as if emphasising what she was talking about. Ashley came out beside Alexis in the dress she had been wearing, It looked much better on Ashley than it ever had on Alexis – it didn't go past Ashley's knees, merely dangled above them and Cassie squealed at her. "You're right you do suit that neckline better. I mean look at Alexis's that dress you picked out for her is amazing" Ashley admired her work with a sharp nod.

Alexis turned around looking for Katie. Expecting the young girl to be somewhere close by but she couldn't see her at this moment.

Alexis could feel her skin crawling as if someone was watching her. She looked up to find the source but nothing seemed to be any different. Alexis turned back to the group who were locked into a conversation. "….You just need the right shoes for that and a necklace, your hair needs to be up" Ashley had pulled Cassie's hair up where it had fallen down. She had turned her to the mirror and was showing her what she meant. "So if we get changed out of these dresses we can get them and then go and get shoes next. KATIE!" Cassie ended shouting on the other girl.

"Coming" Katie seemed harassed but she came out of the other cubical the opposite side of Alexis. She had on a yellow dress. She looked like a princess; it was a corset top with strips of velvet covering her shoulders. The dress was long and puffy at the bottom and it reached down to the floor.

The pink had looked much better on her but she suited the yellow as well. "Very pretty" Ashley mused and Cassie was watching her reaction before speaking. "So you're getting the pink one then?" Cassie asked although it didn't sound much of a question more like a statement which Katie nodded to. "We better all get changed and head to the shoe shop then"

As the girls all descended into their changing rooms, Alexis followed suit and ended up stripping down and putting her clothes back on. She hadn't expected to get much today but the dress was beautiful and if she were going to attend the formal dance she was going to need something to wear.

A shrug moved through Alexis as she grabbed the dress and walked out with it. She could see Ashley already over at the desk, Cassie and Katie must have still been in their cubicles. Alexis headed over to where Ashley was. She walked through the paying process and they put the dress into a beautiful pink and black bag. Cassie was sharp on their heels, and Katie was five minutes after them, her corset dress was obviously harder to get off than the shorter ones.

Once they had all paid for their dresses they headed to the shoe store and got shoes that matched her dress. She got silver strapped shoes that Cassie had picked mostly, Cassie got black high heels that were very simple, Ashley had very big bowed shoes that were also light blue – she also got a pair of stiletto black heels saying she had another dress that would go perfectly with them. Katie didn't get new shoes saying she had already got a perfect pair to go with her dress.

They spent the next few hours going through various other shops, not only for dresses but for bags and accessories.

Alexis didn't have nearly as much as the other two girls had but she had collected up a few dresses and a new t shirt that she had liked with perfecting fitting jeans that flared at the bottom. There had been one feeling that Alexis couldn't shake, she was being watched, at the beginning she had passed it over because they had been trying on clothes and more than likely people would be passing by and looking at them. She didn't think too much of it but after going through store after store she was sure she could feel eyes on her. "Now one more store before we grab something to eat" Cassie announced as she pointed to the store she wanted to go to. "Actually I need to nip to the ladies room, I will catch up with you guys in there" Alexis announced, crossing her fingers that none of the girls would actually go with her. It seemed to be so common with girls to go to the toilet together but luckily for her they all seemed to be enjoying shopping too much.

They waved her off and she rounded the corner and instead of darting left towards the toilets, she moved right and back tracked around herself until she was face to face with the man himself. She knew someone had been following her. Alexis put her hands on her hips. "Caleb! What are you doing here?" Alexis half wondered what was happening, *had Vladimir sent him? Had he come by himself? Why was he even up right now?* He should have been sleeping.

Caleb spun around on his heels and smiled towards Alexis. "You looked so pretty in that dress" Caleb answered causing Alexis to blush slightly; she couldn't let him get away from this or distract her from this. "Leave. Now" Alexis grounded out, pronouncing out each word evenly. She couldn't have him following her around, she didn't know how much longer she was going to be here but she didn't want him following her for all that time.

She was already becoming agitated with him already. "No. Now I didn't get to see the shoes with the dress on. If you don't mind you could show me" Caleb leaned against the side of the wall watching her as if he were being deadly serious, Alexis's mouth opened and shut a few times trying to think of something else to say. "Caleb leave please" Alexis couldn't be bothered with all his nonsense right now they had barely gotten over his last moody instance. "What else did you get? I couldn't get close enough in the underwear store; did you get ones to match?" Caleb inquired with a small smile on his lips.

Alexis blushed a deeper shade of red and tightened her bags against her. "Oh is that them there" He moved as if to get her bags and Alexis tried to keep them away from him. She twisted and turned a few times before she was able to put her hand on his chest and push him back from her. "No you're not seeing what I bought" she shook her head although couldn't remove the blush from her face.

Caleb paused for a moment.

"Ok. I'll leave if you show me everything you've bought when you get back. I want to see them on…" Caleb stopped trying to reach for her bags and folded his arms in front of his chest. This he looked amused at, he waited for her answer and Alexis pondered in her head the problems over what he was saying.

It sounded easy in theory but at the same time only things could go wrong, especially when it was Caleb. Caleb seemed to know exactly the way to manipulate people. He knew exactly what to do. Alexis pursed her lips for a moment before nodding her head. "Fine. Deal" which caused Caleb to grin even wider. "Very well I shall see you at home" He turned to leave and Alexis couldn't believe he was going so easily.

Alexis watched him leave.

This seemed too easy, was he really leaving or was he just trying to trick her into thinking he was leaving. Rolling her eyes she hated the way he made her think of everything. Alexis turned back and moved around the way she was coming, when she came out Cassie, Ashley and Katie were heading out of the shop and waved towards her grabbing her attention. Alexis and the other guys began to head towards the food court, they each got what they wanted and sat down at the table.

Alexis's heart fell through the table when she saw Nicolas in the food court, his eyes caught hers and he waved. Alexis was sure he was going to head over, her hand dipped up to wave and he sat down joining back into his conversation he was in. Alexis smiled slightly sitting down.

"..Was that Nicolas waving to you?" Alexi cringed over Cassie's words and nodded her head and she took a bite of food and a drink of her soda.

24

History Lesson

Lunch with just Nicolas couldn't be that bad an idea. Sure lunch with all the werewolves was scary but with just Nicolas it seemed easier. Nicolas wasn't going to hurt her; he wasn't going to force her to do anything.

Their relationship lately had been slightly different. He had been giving her space, he hadn't been following her about and although he had said *'Hi'* on the passing it wasn't forceful. She hadn't seen much of the werewolves, Sandy had been out of the way, Marie had been friendly and talkative but not constant and she hadn't seen Alex or Patrick at all.

Alexis grabbed her lunch box out of her bag and sat down at the steps outside the building, exactly where they had chosen to meet. It was out of the way from everyone. "Sorry I'm late, the cafeteria is mobbed" Nicolas came out from beside her and sat down. His lunch tray placed on the steps beside him, he picked up something to eat and sighed in delight when he took the first bite. Alexis chuckled slightly "Hungry?" she teased with a smile.

It had become much easier around him the past little while, she didn't seem so nervous. "Starving" Nicolas answered, his eyes watched her brightly and Alexis smiled back towards him. "You're so lovely when you smile" Alexis blushed and looked away on Nicolas's words causing a deep chuckle to go through his chest. "I bet you're a beautiful wolf" Nicolas replied and Alexis stopped smiling the blush instantly moving from her face. She hated when he did this, she hated when he spoiled the moment and brought up her wolf side.

Not that she believed she had a wolf side anymore, she had supressed it so much she doubted it would come out. "You're going to have to acknowledge it sometime." Nicolas answered, his hands were threw his legs and he was leaning forward. "You are a Lupei werewolf after all" Nicolas took a bite out of his sandwich and Alexis's eyebrows knotted together at the top of her forehead.

She was a *what?* A Lupei Werewolf?

Alexis looked at him quizzically which caused Nicolas to look confused for a moment. "You didn't know?" Alexis shook her head when he asked her and Nicolas let out a deep sigh knowing that she really didn't know anything about bèing a werewolf or of who she was in any way shape or form. "That explains so much" He admitted finishing off his sandwich he took a drink. Alexis looked on at him in wonder, how could he know what she was and yet he had never seen her wolf, they had never more than talked to each other and this was the first time they had openly talked with much trouble from everyone else.

It wasn't easy. "How do you know I'm a *Lu-pei*?" Alexis inquired, she had given up on her food and she had placed it down beside her school bag in a step below where she was sitting right now. She had half turned her body towards Nicolas and was truly interested to know what he knew about her. *If he knew, did that mean other people could know?* Alexis worried over that thought in her head. “It’s easy to tell. Especially with your incident with Marie and Sandy.” Nicolas answered intently; he too had given up on the food beside him and had turned his body to face Alexis understanding the importance of this situation for her. He was slightly taller than her, although his limbs were clearly bigger.

Alexis again looked quizzical over the situation and Nicolas smiled slightly. “You ordered them to stop and they did?” He explained, expanding on the situation to see if she could remember. Alexis couldn’t remember the situation but in fact she did remember telling Sandy and Marie to stop. She had thought they had stopped out of surprise, not because they had been made to stop. “You hadn’t’ realised it?” Nicolas inquired into her thoughts and Alexis nodded her head. “I thought they were just surprised I had shouted slightly” Alexis admitted truthfully, she put her hands against her head to think.

It couldn't truly be that bad. She hadn't thought she had ever had control over werewolves before. "So I have control over werewolves?" Alexis asked in wonder and Nicolas watched her reaction, wondering how she felt to that. "Well you're the Alpha wolf species so you have control over other packs of any species of werewolves" Nicolas spoke as if Alexis should have known this although he knew that she didn't.

Her reaction told him as much. "I thought you would have known all this" Nicolas admitted honestly and Alexis again shook her head. "No. I hardly know anything about my wolf side. I actually know nothing about it other than they are dangerous" Alexis shrugged her shoulders knowing that Nicolas didn't agree with her fully on the dangerous side of things. "I suppose that depends on who you speak to on that front. Werewolves are dangerous to every creature other than themselves. Werewolves usually respect each other quiet well especially within their packs. With a few exceptions, if you're wolf was out then Sandy wouldn't be reacting the way she was to you. She would never get the chance too you're wolf would take care of that. We understand the hierarchy just by looking each other in the eye. It's just the way we are as creatures" Nicolas shrugged his shoulders as if he were thinking about why they were the way they are. Alexis watched him in wonder over the situation.

Did that mean that her wolf would threat Sandy's? Alexis couldn't come to grips with the situation at hand. "You're special Alexis. There aren't many werewolves that are Lupei left. You need to be protected" Alexis couldn't deal with Nicolas and his over protectiveness not even in the slightest bit. Nicolas had moved to touch her hands and take them in his. "You need to be under guard" Nicolas finished with pleading eyes.

Alexis didn't want to deal with him at all right now.

She didn't want to see where this was leading. "I am guarded" Alexis wasn't technically lying, she was guarded, she was guarded by Vladimir, Louie and Caleb. They guarded her. She didn't need any more guards, sure Nicolas was a great guy and although he came with a bunch of problems that didn't make him any less of the nice guy. Nicolas seemed relieved at that although at the same time she could see he felt sad. “That’s good to hear” Nicolas murmured softly, his eyes never leaving hers.

“So what happened to the Lupei?” Alexis inquired knowing the story she had heard from Vladimir and Daniel to be true but at the same time she wanted to hear what had happened to the Lupei werewolves from someone other than the vampire in her life.

Nicolas watched her carefully for a moment before looking away and started his story. “We don’t know first-hand what happened after all I was only three or four when they were completely killed off. But as far as I know the vampires started to hunt down every Lupei pack and kill them off. It started with the smaller packs and then they worked up to their main Alpha pack. The Alpha was weakened because his wife had just died during childbirth and the child had died as well. He had a son and a daughter already but he was grief stricken and although he tried to protect his kids, he stood no chance – his mate had died.

You don't get over that so easily." Nicolas was sad as if he were thinking of something else in his life. Nicolas had lost his mother which was his father's mate; he had listened to his father talk about his mother which such happiness and pain, he had never found that same love ever again. There was only ever one soul mate for each person and Nicolas was determined not to lose his like his father had lost his mother. "As far as all the other packs were concerned they had killed off every Lupei werewolf but you change that fact. A Lupei has the strongest gene against any werewolf. If you had children they would be Lupei werewolves no matter who you were mated too. That means you have the power to save the Lupei line" Nicolas still hadn't looked towards her although he told his story clear, his voice trying not to waver in any way shape or form. *Was he telling the truth?*

Sure the story was similar to the one Alexis had heard, she knew the werewolves had been killed off by the vampires because they had thought them to be too dangerous. "Why did the vampires attack them?" Alexis inquired ignoring most of the second part of what Nicolas had said. She couldn't deal with this at the moment but she could deal with the stuff she was finding out about her species. It matched Vladimir's too some extent but the details were changed slightly.

One was towards the vampires; making them look like the hero's, the other was towards the werewolves – making them look like they had been slaughtered. Alexis didn't know what to believe or to say to that. Nicolas shrugged. "I've heard so many stories I don't know which one is true. Some say it was just to try and weaken the werewolf species by taking out our Alpha's – the Farkas are a group of werewolves which are out of control and the Lupei kept them in line – without them they believed the Farkas would go insane. Luckily enough someone is bringing them towards a treaty which will keep them under control. Then I've heard that it would make the rest of the werewolves fight for the top spot but none want to take the Lupei's position.

They were believed to be able to talk to our ancestors and decipher the right path to take. No other species have that kind of power" Nicolas shrugged slightly finally looking towards her.

Alexis was deep in thought. She couldn't work out what was happening. Nicolas pulled Alexis's hands close to his body trying to grab her attention. "You don't need to worry about the past, not anymore. You need to think to the future. It's all that matters" Nicolas offered a kind smile which Alexis tried to give him back. He did make her feel a little bit better although not completely.

She was still trying to work out what was the truth, Vampires of course would protect themselves in stories but Werewolves would do the same. *Who would actually tell her the truth? Who could she trust?* Alexis shook her head trying to clear her thoughts. Nicolas grabbed her chin and faced it towards him. "Don't over think everything. It will be okay. You will work everything out through time. Lupei's have a long life span" Nicolas answered back, that didn't make her feel any better. He knew more about her species than she did. He knew more about her than she did. Nicolas smile leaning closer towards her. *What was he doing?* Alexis's eyes widened slightly when she realised he was moving closer towards her.

He was going to kiss her. *Did she want him to kiss her?* Should she let him kiss her? So many thoughts were moving through her head and all the while her eyes were focused on his lips, her back was moving backwards slightly. "ALEXIS!" The words echoed to both of them and Alexis sprung up, leaving Nicolas growling slightly as he looked to the owner of the voice.

Cassie, he tried to readjust himself and change the look on his face and eventually he offered her a nice smile. "Cassie. Whats up?" Alexis bounced from one foot to the next, running her hands through her hair. *What had she almost done? What was she going to do?* Cassie smiled brightly not caring for the situation in front of her she linked hands with Alexis and turned to Nicolas. "I need to borrow this one if you don't mind" Cassie inquired towards Nicolas in which he waved his hand. "Just remember to bring her back" Nicolas teased, his eyes moving over Alexis once before Cassie squealed and moved with Alexis back towards the school.

"We have got to get ready for my 18th and you have got to wear that dress you bought on Friday! – It was so pretty on you"

Cassie pulled Alexis away and Alexis couldn't help but cast her eyes back to look towards the werewolf. He had almost kissed her.

She didn't know how she felt about that. She was glad Cassie had interrupted – she couldn't deal with more difficult relationships right now. She was finding it hard enough dealing with Caleb at her own house.

25

Hot session

"Left" the yell echoed through her ears as if it were bursting her ear drum, but she obeyed it and swung her left hand forward into the bag in front of her. She felt the rumble hit her hand and then echo all the way up her shoulder. She would never get the hang of punching. She flinched and pulled her hand back against her chest covering it with her other hand. "Ouch" she couldn't help the involuntary screech that left her lips. She had said it many times in the past hour and no matter how many times she would punch the bag, it still hurt. She was in the gym but she had spent most of the hour in this position punching the bag.

A matt under her feet held her steady and gave her comfort, although not much. “Stop putting your thumb under your fingers. That’s why it hurts” his strong voice over powered her like it did every time he spoke and he came towards her this time grabbing her hand away from her chest and showing her how to do it.

His hands were cold to touch but she didn’t flinch away from then. She felt the surge of electricity run through her like every time he touched her. She froze and allowed him to uncurl her hand, pushing her thumb out and then curling her fingers back in. “This is how you have to keep your hand unless you want to break your hand when you punch” Caleb softly pushed out, his voice holding a gentler tone, nicer than before.

One she had grown used to hearing when he was more relaxed. His normal blue eyes stared up at her telling her, he did care for her, he did want to help her before it was gone in seconds. He pushed her hand away and moved from her faster than her eyes could follow. “We’ll do some matt work and then you can get back to your homework.” He spoke from the middle of the room and she whirled around to see him fixing the matts. The room was big and completely covered in a wooden floor but on top of the floor was 26 matts, faded blue in colour.

Scattered around the edges of the room were benches and seats where both her jumper and bag sat and his extra clothes and bottle of blood was. She hated the fact that she knew that; that she knew what was in his bottle and it didn't scare her.

It didn't creep her out. It should have.

She nodded her head and moved herself over towards him. He began to stretch out his limbs, normally he had done that before she had even reached the gym, so she was quiet surprised when he bent forward and touched his toes and began jogging on the spot. He walked through everything as if he had his own routine, as if he didn't need to think about what he was doing.

Alexis stood to the side and watched him not knowing whether she should join in – she was sure she would look stupid trying to be herself, she didn't know if her body would actually bend. She was stiff, she had only just started exercising with Caleb, it was the first she had been doing in a long while, she hadn't exactly been good in keeping her fitness up, she was good with books and studying just like Vladimir and Louie were.

She stared on in amazement as he stretched out every one of his limbs "Are you going to join in?" She shook her head trying to gain her attention back on the situation at hand, she must have dazed in thought. Her vision came back to her and Caleb stood not that far from her, watching her curiously. She quickly recovered stepping forward on to the matt and tried to act like she hadn't just drifted off into her own head.

"What are we doing first?" she charged straight into work knowing they had already gone over the basics, everything from falling to punching right. He must have wanted to mix some of it together; he often tried to put her into to fighting position to see how she would react in them. "We're going to see how much you've learned over the weeks" Caleb said basically moving in front of her, a little bit closer and getting into a fighting position. "Attack and defend, use everything I have taught you and don't hold back. You can't hurt me" Caleb joked although he smiled it was half-heartedly.

Alexis nodded her head and smiled back at him, pushing her feet in to the balance position he had taught her. She knew he was going to hold back, after all he had a lot more strength than her, but then again he had made sure to teach her how to combat certain types of strength.

Once she was ready she nodded her head and he fired out with a punch which she was ready for.

It hit her but hardly, she was able to curve it to the side. Again he started moving punches towards her which she was able to detour, he moved to the side and she moved with him, she could hold her balance while moving, he had taught her that the fourth time they had got together. When Caleb started to bounce on his feet instead of punching she took it as her chance to attack – she swung her hand out to punch him as a distraction and when he dodged it she bent to her floor, and swiped her feet underneath him. He jumped and she bounced to her feet knowing he had spoken about being vulnerable on the ground.

She took a blow to the stomach when she stood up before she could get her balance back, but she was able to block the next punch he sent her way by dodging to the left.

Alexis was smiling and Caleb couldn't help but take it easier on her just for that very reason. "You're not meant to smile at your attacker" Caleb pointed out and Alexis tried to put the smile off of her face, although it was difficult to think of Caleb as her '*attacker*'. Caleb smirked at her attempt to look serious and she started bouncing on her feet trying to think of her next move to attack him.

"Ready?" She questioned a smile trying to be pulled off of her face as she teased him, his eyes rolled and he moved into a defensive position making everything seem more dramatic than what it was. She bounced on her feet again, getting herself ready for action and ready to pounce on him.

She didn't announce she was coming; she bounced on the spot a few more times making sure that he didn't know she was coming before she took a few steps forward and tripped towards him the rest of the way. Her face fell from its usual smile and he wasn't fast enough to readjust himself, he wasn't even aware she had stopped running until she bashed into him and he fell to the ground. Her body landed on top of his, her head crashing into his chest and his back curled as he landed. His hands came around Alexis to make sure she wouldn't get hurt, as an automatic reaction.

Caleb's eyes had closed and when he gathered himself, he looked down his chin to Alexis's head. Alexis was vibrating, her body was moving in slow up and down movements.

Caleb braced himself, he couldn't see her, and he couldn't tell if she was ok. "Alexis?" his words questioned her and he tried to turn his head to see if he could see her. Her head pulled up after a minute or two and he could finally see what she was feeling.

She was laughing. He frowned watching her, although his body relaxed knowing she was okay. "I can't believe I just tripped" Alexis smirked as she looked at him, her body shaking with laughter that she couldn't sit up; she managed to at least look at him balancing her hands slightly on the ground. "….And even worse you didn't catch me." Alexis laughed again as she couldn't believe that not only had she fallen but a vampire hadn't been able to catch her and he had ended up down on the ground with her.

Caleb frowned towards her and Alexis tilted her head into his chest again to mask her laughter. "That's not funny" Caleb tried to push out with a serious face, although with Alexis laughing in front of him he couldn't keep a completely straight face, her laugh was rippling through his chest. She nodded her head as if answering his question with that simple gesture. When she lifted her head this time her face was closer to his, his eyes watched her in curiosity. "You're supposed to be some big ass vampire and you couldn't even keep me or yourself from falling"

Another burst of laughter echoed out through her lips as she faced him. Her laugh was faulted when she felt herself being flipped over and her back was on the ground, Caleb lay above her, his arms holding his body wait over her. A creepy yet alluring smile placed over his face and she couldn't help but stare into his now, black eyes. "Did no one ever teach you not to tease a vampire?" Caleb's voice was deep and seductive, his breath was heavy and she could feel it on her face.

Alexis's look went from playful to serious in seconds.

A smirk went across his face as if he could sense the change in her. His head moved closer to hers, and her heart rate picked up. He let out a small chuckle that rumbled through his chest. "I'm a very dangerous creature you know" He spoke although he was so close to Alexis that she hardly felt like breathing, he dipped his head closer to his neck and her hands tightened on his sides, anxious. His eyes were black and eventually Alexis found herself staring at the ceiling, her heart skipped a beat as his breath found his way to her neck. "You don't want to be on my bad side" his voice was close to her ear and she held her breath as his teeth scrapped across her neck, sharp.

Was he going to bite her? No he wouldn't. Would he? Her thoughts fought against themselves and she focused all her energy on holding her breath and wondering if he was going to bite her. His head moved and her eyes shut tight wondering if this was it.

If he was going to bite her, she wasn't sure how she felt about that. She waited for his teeth to break her skin but instead she felt a small pressure against her neck, as he pressed his lips at the curve. When her eyes opened, he was pushed above her assessing her reaction with a devilish smile placed along his lips. "You're an ass" she pushed at him trying to get away from him.

He let out a laugh and after a moment he pushed off of her and stood to his feet offering her a hand to get up, she grabbed his hands and he lifted her up with ease. "You enjoyed it though" he pointed out, her face blushed and she made a frustrated sound and moved to the door.

She had really thought he was going to bite her, not only that she wasn't even sure how she felt about that, although she had enjoyed his closeness and then he had spoiled that with his cocky attitude.

Like he always did.

A laugh echoed behind her as she grabbed her jumper and headed out the door and away from him.

26

Something sour on the menu

Marie stood in front of Alexis, her eyes pleaded with the young girl. She wanted to persuade her to do the right thing, after all Nicolas was her mate. Marie wanted to get a good relationship going with her especially if she was going to be the next female to lead the pack. She was much nicer than Sandy and Marie could already tell that they could be good friends.

"I promise we're not all bad. You've not even met half of the pack. We're just the ones that attend this school, another five attend the school on the opposite side of our reservation and then there are the younger ones who we have a school on our lands and the older ones who attend college and their parents and the adults that work. You're just dealing with high school kids who are bad enough as humans without adding werewolves into the mix. Please have lunch with us. I promise it won't be bad and you can leave at any time." She pleaded with Alexis; Alexis looked at her with an awkward smile. She didn't want to sit with a group of werewolves but at the same time perhaps if she did sit with them and she explained to them that she didn't want to join their pack and that she was only here to study then perhaps they would get the picture.

Perhaps they would leave her alone.

Alexis pondered the thought for a moment before nodding her head. She didn't trust her voice to say anything. Marie smiled happily; jumping up and down for a moment Alexis was surprised by the girls reaction. Marie grabbed her hand and began to drag her forward "Good we got seats outside today because of the weather. Everyone's going to be so happy to see you" *Wait! They didn't know?* Alexis suddenly felt panicked; she had thought the wolves asking her to lunch had been a joint decision. She knew it wouldn't have been Sandy's idea but the rest possibly might have agreed to it.

Alexis suddenly felt like she was being dragged along the corridor towards the outside. She waved at a passing Cassie and tried to act like she was going willingly outside.

Although it felt very difficult to do considering the circumstances. “Relax, Alexis. It’s going to be fine” Marie spoke before she pushed the door open and ushered Alexis out with her. Alexis laughed nervously, wondering how she can possible relax under these circumstances. She was about to have lunch with all these werewolves. She wasn’t sure if she was happy bringing her own lunch anymore, at least if she had to go and get her lunch it would be an excuse for her to leave.

Now she felt trapped. “Hey guys!” Marie waved dragging Alexis along behind her as they approached the wolves. Nicolas perked up, he was sat on the table with his feet on the seat, either side of him was Rick and Alexander but they had to turn to see Alexis and Marie coming. Rick smiled seeing Marie although didn’t react much more than that. Alexander just stared on at them slightly amused. Alexis half wondered what he was amused at.

Nicolas stood to his feet to greet the girls, with a smile on his face. "Look who decided to join us for lunch" Marie smiled turning towards Alexis and Alexis had to resist the urge to roll her eyes. It was hardly her decision but instead she smiled and sheepishly said "Hi" Nicolas was the first to step up and smile towards her. "Alexis, It's nice to see you" Nicolas breathed out and Alexis nodded her head, her cheeks staining red as Marie pulled her to sit down on the steps behind the boys.

Rick handed Marie a tray with some food on it as Alexis dug into her bag for her lunch, although she didn't feel like she could eat it. Her stomach was acting out, it was tossing and tumbling. She did, however, feel like her throat was so dry, she grabbed her drink pulling it out and taking a drink out of it. "So have you always stayed around here?" Alexander blurted out casing Nicolas to nudge him and Rick to shake his head. Marie stared at Alexander with a glare and Alexis swallowed before answering, her head shook. "No. Only about three years. I used to stay around Europe for a little while and I started in New York before that" Alexis answered honestly, knowing that saying things like that wouldn't compromise her in any way shape or form. After all she couldn't exactly come out and say she stayed with vampires. It wouldn't go down well, especially with werewolves. Alexander nodded his head as if confirming what she had said.

The other's looked at Alexis as if surprised she had answered the question. Marie smiled beside her. "So were you born in New York?" she inquired hoping that Alexis's sharing was going to continue. They were searching for information on which pack she was from, Alexis already knew that. Although she wasn't sure what she could say to them.

"No I moved there when I was three or four" Alexis spoke as she took another drink of her juice trying to quench a thirst that wasn't there. But at the same time if they were asking her question's there was no shame in her asking them questions. "Have you always stayed around here?" She inquired to any of them, knowing she didn't care who answered it really. She just wanted to make conversation and find out if they lived closely around here.

She didn't think Vladimir would have moved her somewhere near a werewolf pack but then again maybe he didn't know. The Elders seemed to always know where they were as well so didn't that mean they should always check where they put Alexis? She wondered but shook it off. "We've resided here for generations" Nicolas was the one to answer and while Alexis tried not to look at him, it was becoming increasingly difficult.

Alexis nodded her head; it seemed someone must have known about the nearby packs. "And you've been home-schooled up until now, right?" Rick asked and Alexis nodded her head agreeing with the statement. "My guardian's thought it would be easier than moving me around schools all the time" Alexis stated, nobody had touched the food in front of them since Alexis and the wolves had started speaking.

They all seemed to be slightly nervous in their in own way. "You're Guardian's?" Nicolas was the one to question it and Alexis cursed herself for not wording that differently. *Why had she had to mention she had guardians?* She supposed the question would have been asked sooner or later. Alexis again nodded her head although didn't say anything causing Alexander to look towards Nicolas wondering if they should inquire any further.

Nicolas shook his head.

They didn't want to push Alexis away especially when they had just gotten her to sit down and speak to them, which seemed like a challenge all on its own. "Cassie said you asked to come for your last year of school" Marie stated as if not only talking to Alexis but telling the boys that fact as well. Alexis nodded her head again. "I've not interacted much with people and although my Guardian's made a good school environment I wanted to see it for myself and see other people's opinions" Alexis admitted.

Which she knew was something that Caleb didn't understand and she wasn't sure if these wolves were going to understand it either. Vladimir acted as if he understood and Louie – well Louie acted as if he didn't care as long as he got to see Alexis.

Marie opened her mouth to speak again but something caught her eye and she turned to see what it was.

Sandy.

Sandy was moving towards them, she was dressed in much shorter clothes than she usually did. Alexis hadn't looked up; she was still awkwardly looking down. Nicolas hadn't looked up either; he was staring at Alexis in wonder. *Who were these guardians that she was talking about? Were they werewolves? Or something else?* Nicolas was curious.

Sandy's short skirt left very little to the imagination and her shirt that showed her stomach and most of her breasts. Sandy paraded in to their group with no bother; she acted as if there was no difference now than there ever was before. Alexis head moved up when she heard Nicolas's voice. "Sandy?" It sounded concerned and Alexis couldn't help but look up. She wanted to fight the reaction but found she couldn't.

Marie gasped beside her and Alexander growled. Sandy had barged in and was now sitting on Nicolas's lap although Nicolas didn't look happy about that. She sat on one of his knees with a smile spread on her lips as if she didn't know what was wrong with this situation. She swung her arms around his neck and snuggled against him, for some reason Alexis felt as if her body was on fire.

Her throat scratched as if it wanted to growl, she refused to let that reaction come out of her. She found herself looking away again "Did….How…So did it take you a while to find the right school is that why you didn't start at the beginning of last term?" Marie tried to look away from the scene in front of her and ignore what was going on. She looked towards Alexis who wasn't the only person who felt awkward. Alexander beside Nicolas was facing away from the group, he looked angry and Rick had shifted himself slightly away from Nicolas.

Nicolas was growling low in his throat although that didn't seem to bother Sandy at all. She just whispered something in his ear. Alexis needed to get out of here. She stood to her feet, hesitating making an excuse towards the wolves or just taking off. Her manners getting the better of her. "I need to go find Cassie before class" She hesitated again wondering if that was enough to allow her to leave before she turned away from the wolves and started to leave.

"Lexi" Nicolas's voice was calling out to her and he had finally stood up pushing Sandy off of him – Sandy refused to fully let go of him though. She was sure she wasn't going to let him follow her. Alexander had moved from his seat though and had followed after Alexis.

Alexis was pulled back by her arm. Alexander had grabbed it. She was shocked as she stood staring at him. "Don't just leave like that!" his voice sounded angry and Alexis tried to pull her arm back towards herself. She didn't know what to say and she was sure that no matter what she said it wasn't going to calm Alexander down, Alexis was scared. "She's not a threat to you and she couldn't hurt you with us there" Alexander tightened his grip on her arm causing Alexis to squeal slightly. "Let go" Alexis finally found the words to speak, causing Alexander to let go of her suddenly, frowning.

It was as if he hadn't realised he was holding her so tightly. When he let go Alexis pulled her arm close and rubbed where he had been holding. Alexis watched him and Alexander seemed to grimace at his actions. He hadn't meant to do that. Alexis could see that by the look in his eyes. He was as surprised as her by what he had done. *Could he not control his own actions?* "Lex, don't go" Nicolas voice was behind them and when Alexis moved to see him, Alexander took off.

What was wrong with him? Alexis's thought followed as her gaze watched after the temperamental wolf. He was a curious one indeed. "I'm sorry about that. I really am" Nicolas had caught up to her and now stood in front of her.

Luckily the bell chose that point to ring causing them both to face the school although neither moved. Alexis shook her head. "There's nothing to be sorry for." Alexis admitted, which in every case was true. Nicolas wasn't hers and they weren't dating. Sandy had every right to be all over him, in fact she had more than every right. She was dating him first.

In fact if it wasn't for Alexis she would still be dating him. Nicolas shook his head and took a step towards Alexis trying to grab her hand. Alexis shook him off. "I need to get to class, please just leave me alone" Alexis spoke sadly before she turned to leave.

The werewolves were unstable, if Nicolas was Alpha and he couldn't even control how Sandy acted around him then it was obvious there was a lack of authority. Nicolas watched his mate leave with restraint. "Alexis!" he called after her and she waved her hand at him. "Nico please!" she didn't have the energy nor the time to say his full name. She had regretted it as soon as she had said, she didn't want to call him a nickname, and she didn't want to call him anything else. She just wanted to get rid of him.

Although that didn't seem to be working. It took everything in him not to chase after her and make her feel better. He wanted to comfort her and he wanted to protect her but he didn't seem to be doing any of that lately. He needed to find a way to show her how she made him feel. He needed to prove to her that he was her mate. He just didn't know how he was going to show her right now. His dad had mentioned many things about your *mate* and he was trying to recall all of them right now.

The feelings he had talked about.

The actions, the protectiveness. *The kiss?*

Nicolas knew as soon as he said the word that it was the only thing he could do. He needed to show her with a kiss.

27

Heightened complication

She stood outside the school, the cold wind running through her hair. The building towered over her and covered some of the sunshine that was covering the school yard. Her hand gripped her bag tight against her and she strained past all the students flooding away from the school to try and find her ride, Vladimir. He wasn't here yet and he was never normally too late.

Sure a few times he had waited till the school to clear before he had turned up but lately he just stopped the car near the school and Alexis would jump in.

A sigh left her lips as her eyes drew away from the parking lot and its mobbed covered students. What she faced when she turned around though wasn't much better.

Nicolas Maori.

He looked like he was on a mission and Alexis could not have him standing around while she was waiting on Vladimir. She had got this far without Vladimir knowing she wasn't about to be caught out. She tried to turn slightly ignoring him, hoping he would take the hint. But apparently he did not, Nico stopped beside her, not saying anything as if waiting for her to say something first. "Nico…." She groaned turning towards him, at any other time she could have ignored him – she could have walked away but with Vladimir on his way she couldn't risk it.

The wind picked up her hair and she turned herself away from the sun so she could see better; the building still held all its beauty from no matter what angle she was in. It was great, it was red sandstone in all its glory and Alexis couldn't help but admire it. "I'm not leaving you here by yourself, Lex" Nicolas's arms folded across his chest and he gazed out into the parking lot as if expecting someone else to come for her.

"Stop calling me that. My name is A-lex-is" she snapped back needing a reason to get rid of him. "What do you prefer? I can go with Lexi if that's better, or Alex. I am sure we will find one that suits you better with time – one that is just mine…." Nico was teasing her, baiting her into talking to him just like he did every time they talked. He wanted a reaction. Any reaction out of her.

He was trying to make a point and she wasn't going to listen to it. She wasn't going to deal with this. She couldn't deal with this; not now. "Nico just leave" Although he was shaking his head before she'd even finished talking. He wasn't going to leave that easily and she should have known that. He was here for a purpose; one that Alexis didn't want to indulge in – she turned away from him trying to ignore the wolf. Something had to get him to leave. "You don't even understand who I am too you!" Nico threw his hands up in desperation, before pulling them through his hair. He tried not to strain his voice, considering they were in front of the school.

The grounds were just now clearing of kids and yet Nico refused to leave Alexis by herself and not only that, but he refused to let this matter go. He believed he was her mate. *Her wolf mate.* "Nico, I hardly know you" Alexis tried to speak straight and tried also not to look at him. She found it easier to concentrate and stay in control over a conversation when she didn't look at him.

Which was becoming increasingly difficult as he walked in circles trying to get her attention to focus on him. "I have only just met you" Alexis again spoke her head shaking and her arms folding across her chest as she prayed for Vladimir to hurry up and pick her up. She hated a Thursday when she had to stick around the school and wait for Vlady to pick her up.

Every other day she had that driver he had hired – but on Thursday it was his days off and Vladimir had insisted he come and get her. He was always late, Alexis hated it – it was always a chance for Nico or one of the wolves to try and talk to her more. She had successfully avoided a confrontation up until now. “I am your mate, Lex” Nico grabbed her shoulders and made her stare at him. Her eyes met his and she refused to melt into them.

They were pleading her to listen to him; to believe what he was saying was true. But how could she. She didn’t feel the same way as he did and she couldn’t, she had suppressed her wolf gene. With a deep sign, Alexis shook her head and looked down. *How could she believe him?* She couldn’t be bound to wolves; they were nasty horrible creatures that killed people.

Sure – it didn’t seem like Nico and his pack was like that but that didn’t mean that every werewolf was good. *How could she just forget what she was brought up believing?* She couldn’t. She trusted Vladimir and he couldn’t have lied to her. He wouldn’t lie to her. Nico’s fingers tilted her chin back up and before she knew what was happening her lips were pressed against his.

Hard. For a moment she melted, her full body felt like crumbling under him and just giving in, a niggle at the back of her mind just begging her to give in, to let it consume her. Let him consume her. She had been fighting it all her life, she would always ignore it.

It took only a few seconds for her to grab her full attention away from Nico again. Her eyes shot up ad she pressed her hands against his chest pushing him backwards. She forced herself to be strong, forced herself to put all her strength into pushing him away from her. She didn't want this. She wanted to avoid this and she was going to get him off of her. Her head shook and she took a step backwards when she couldn't push him off.

He let her go. She didn't think he would but he did. He let her slip out of his reach and although his eyes searched hers for any answers that would let him in, he was disappointed. He wanted more than anything for her to give in. For her to accept that she was *his* mate. But she couldn't feel that, she didn't see the same thing he did. Her head shook and she felt close to tears.

The wind around them only seemed to pick up; she could feel it running through all her hairs which at the moment were stood on end. "I can't" Alexis muttered, her voice wavering as she lowered her eyes so she wasn't looking at him, her head was shaking as she spoke trying to make herself believe it.

Nico took a step towards her making sure her hands were in his and that she looked at him before speaking. He wanted her to understand, he wanted her to listen to the words he was about to say. "You will. When you're ready. When you let *Lupus* come out. You'll feel it" Nico pronounced out each word and made sure he meant it. He made sure that Alexis understood him. *That word? Why did he call her wolf a name?* She had never known anyone to call her wolf that. Her eyes watched him before switching to the side.

Caleb stood outside a car staring exactly in the direction they were standing in. Alexis could almost see him about to explode. *How much had he seen? How long had he been there?* She didn't need to even ask that. He had seen it all, she felt it. He had been there when Nico kissed her. She pulled her hands out of Nico's, looked once more at him before turning around and running towards Caleb.

“Cal, don’t get mad” Nico watched her run off and he felt the growl vibrate out of him with anger. A vampire? The question hung in his head as he watched them. *His mate.* The wolf in his mind was furious with possessiveness, it scratched at his skin begging to be let out, to let him take care of this situation. It made his hair stand on end and his body heat up to endless extent. His wolf had never fought for anything so hard in its life.

It always stayed hidden unless he asked it to help. Unless he needed to help, normally he could sense it. But this time it was completely different, it was trying to take charge of his body with force. As if the wolf believed he couldn’t handle the situation himself. He couldn’t let it, not here. He would protect Alexis and he would get her back. But he had to be patient, he would have to keep his wolf tamed and under control for now.

We will have our time. He told his wolf and he could feel it calming down just with his words. Caleb was full of anger, it was radiating off of him and when she spoke he opened the door for her, signalling for her to get in. He wasn’t discussing this with her in the middle of the car park. The black car was sleek when she slid into it, his leather seats seem to make her feel so small.

Caleb shut the door behind her and she jumped, he was around the side of the car quicker than he should have been in front of humans, or even werewolves. *This is going to be an interesting car journey*; she cowered down in her chair not knowing what to say in this situation. She didn't know how to start a conversation, she wasn't sure how much he had seen and she was sure no matter how much he had seen it wasn't good. She had betrayed him in his eyes; she had gone behind his back. She had gone behind all the vampires back – she wasn't going to be back at school again now. Not when Vladimir and Louie found out.

They wouldn't let her near wolves, no matter how nice she said they were.

Not that she thought ALL the wolves were nice, Alexander certainly wasn't a cup of tea and Sandy had done everything in her power to get rid of her. She hoped the beta wolf was happy now. She was finally going to get her wish.

Alexis wasn't going to be allowed back to high school, she didn't even know if she was going to lose Caleb as well. She tried to keep her feelings away from both boys, and yet in the end she was going to end up losing both Caleb and Nicolas. Friends. Her only friends, she was going to lose the two only friends she had made her age. Her head hung in silence and Caleb took off.

28

Inner battle, lost?

The car ride home was silent although you could have cut the tension with a knife. Alexis didn't know what to say, she didn't know how to say it. He had watched her kissing Nicolas. It was the first time, sure and even if that had been a shock to her, she didn't think it would have made any difference to Caleb.

She had kissed a werewolf. His mortal enemy.

The thoughts going through her head was torturing her and she was curious about his thoughts. He was in turmoil, he couldn't sit still but yet he didn't want to move, his hands felt like they wanted to break something, his teeth felt like they wanted to burst out his mouth and his eyes were trying hard to focus on anything but Alexis heartbeat. She was *his.* She felt like his. It was hard to explain why and he was sure if he had tried to explain it to her she would have laughed or have been insulted. He couldn't explain it to her.

To him, she was his fully, all of her and what she had done had angered him. Not only because it was a werewolf but because she had kissed someone else. It didn't matter what creature it was. He had trusted her; he had put himself out there. All he could hear was Daniel's words in his head '*never trust anyone, especially someone you are attracted to'*.

If Daniel knew any of this, he would have a field day. He would no doubt make Caleb drain Alexis just for the fun of it. Daniel had made a big effort to keep Caleb out of Love and concentrated on the Lust side of things and now on his first job alone he had done exactly what he had been trained not to do. He was stupid. Alexis couldn't even begin to understand what he was going through. That stupid werewolf should never have been near her outside that building, she should have stayed away from him like she had promised herself she would. She didn't want to start a fight and she wanted to confine in Caleb. But how did she tell Caleb that.

He seemed so upset and angry about it. Her head reeled with the possibilities of what had just happened. Her lips still tasted of him – she was lucky that Caleb couldn't read her mind. They were flying along the streets at a speed Alexis was sure was illegal. She didn't want to point that out though, she couldn't even find the light hearted tone she would usually use with Caleb. He was far too angry for that. His impossibly tight grip on the steering wheel only proved that.

The moving houses and shops outside couldn't even distract her from what was happening in the car – they were all a blur. *What could she say to break this tension? Was he not going to say anything?* She had a bond with Caleb – they both knew that but it had hardly been spoken about, mostly avoided. They had never even shared a kiss– there was no wonder he was angry.

He had started to trust Alexis and now it looked like she was throwing it back in his face. *How could she explain what had happened?* She had never even told them there were werewolves in the school. That was already a distrustful thing.

Not to mention the kiss….The car was forced to a stop and Alexis was glad she had strapped in, her chest was thrown forward and then pulled back by the seat belt as they stopped in front of the house they both resided in.

What now?

Alexis sat still not wanting to make the first move afraid of how he might react. But Caleb had a completely different idea. He was already taking his seat belt off and getting himself out of the car. Alexis did the only thing she could think of. She followed him. She followed him out of the car and into the house.

She let the door shut behind her scared that he would disappear if she took her eyes off of him for a moment. She didn't want to be the first to talk but she wasn't sure if he was going to say anything to her…*What if he never spoke to her again? How could she deal with that?* She needed to speak to him, she needed him. Her mouth opened to speak, but was quickly closed when he spoke first. “How can you even…” Caleb threw his hands up in frustration; he couldn’t find the words to say. He didn’t know how to say it.

Of course she was attracted to her own kind. She was a werewolf, no matter how many times she supressed her gene. She was always going to be a werewolf. *How could he have ever thought otherwise?* He thought she had cared for him. He thought he could have opened up to her, could have cared for her, could have lo…no he could never have loved her.

He couldn’t even say the words. Not know, not after what she had done. “Caleb!” She squealed at him again, trying to grab his attention. He was marching through the house and she was trying to catch up with him. The house corridors seemed to be getting longer and longer but he didn’t seem to be slowing down any until he stopped dead and turned on her. His eyes seemed darker than they had ever been before.

“You kissed a werewolf Alexis!”

His voice was no louder than he usually spoke. He wasn’t raising it; he was just adding anger behind it. Alexis felt like it made him a completely different person. The dimly lit blue corridor seemed to be closing in on her. He seemed a lot taller than he usually did. “He kissed me” her voice was weak and she knew she shouldn’t have said anything like that. She didn’t need to defend herself against a vampire, but she did feel like she needed to defend herself against Caleb.

He wasn’t just a vampire. She cared for him and she would have never intentionally kissed Nicolas, not that she wasn’t attracted to him either but she wasn’t ready to kiss anyone well enough a werewolf. She had just got used to the fact of being in a school with werewolves. But the words she used just seemed to make him worse. “You don’t just let someone kiss you Alexis. You’re a strong girl. You have made that obvious enough. You don’t let someone kiss you if you don’t want them too” His head shook and he couldn’t even find the courage to look at her anymore.

He was disgusted, his body was beginning to shake and he leaned on the wall beside him, hoping it would provide him with some balance. Alexis didn’t want to move – no that was a lie she wanted to move out of his way, but she couldn't get her legs to obey her. She couldn't find the strength to push them in another direction. She wanted to comfort him but didn't know how to. His breathing was getting heavier and she could see his fangs prodding out the side of his lips. Her heart beat began to pick up and she was sure he had noticed. His ears had tensed up and his natural instinct was trying to take over. She took in a deep breathing hoping to calm herself as she reach an arm out to touch him, to comfort him.

As soon as her hand touched him she was thrown backwards, his speed was something she had never seen before, his eyes were as black as night as he stood over her. Alexis's cheek was in pain, a bright red mark shaped like a hand was pushed over it. She wanted to reach up and touch it, to conceal it but found that it was still a little stingy to the touch.

One hand held her up on the wooding floor. Caleb stood crouched over her completely terrifying. His fangs were dominating his mouth and his crouched position looked like he was ready to attack her. What felt like an age had only been seconds before Caleb shook his head and his face returned to normal, his blue eyes faded back in from the black and his back straighten.

Across his face was not a predatory look but in fact a look of shock and guilt. *What had he done? What had he let himself do?* He felt like a monster. He hadn't contained himself like he had done for all these years. *How had this happened? What was she doing to him?* He had never lost control before; he had never felt so much emotion. He was supposed to be a vampire, a cold and dark creature that fed on the living – not care about it. How was this even possible? Daniel had warned him about this. Daniel was going to kill him, or worse. He shook his head again trying to shake some sense into himself before he stormed off past her, leaving her lying on the ground.

He couldn't help her, he couldn't touch her again, and he wouldn't trust himself too. He didn't know what he would do. She was safer herself. Her cheek bright red and her head still reeling with the shock. She couldn't hold it back; tears began to burst from her eyes like a waterfall as she picked herself up from the ground and ran to her room. It felt so far away yet she was there within moments.

Pushing her head into her pillow to mask the sound.

She had lost both of them.

29

The truth will set you free

A chap on her door echoed through her mind and she lifted her head to it.

Was this Caleb coming to say sorry? She shouldn't expect so much of him but she couldn't help but hope. He had hit her, she couldn't believe it but the red mark that spread across her face spoke more than words could ever say. She could still feel the pain vibrating through her cheek. But the culprit didn't come in. Whoever it was stood waiting at the door for her answer. Her head ached, something scratched at the surface and she shook her head trying to ignore it. "Come in" Her voice was dull and chocked up, she had been crying, anybody could hear that in her voice. She wiped her eyes clear and sat up on the edge of her bed as a tall and striking Vladimir came in. He looked sullen, his eyes were sad and his head lowered. She could barely make out his eyes as she watched him.

"Are you alright?" He questioned lifting his head a touch to be able to see her better. Her eyebrows scrunched up in wonder, *what did he have to be sad about? Did he blame himself for letting Caleb in to the house and injuring her?* He shouldn't have.

Alexis had learned enough about Caleb to know he had a short temper and sure she hadn't expected him to turn up at her school but she hadn't ever been so close to Nicolas before. That had been the first time. He had pulled her into a kiss thinking that it would prove to her that he was her mate and yet it had only made things worse.

It had only gotten her more in trouble. Alexis head nodded and she tried to half smile at him. "What can I say? Louie was right, Caleb does have a temper" Alexis shrugged trying to make it seem less important than it actually was believing that was why Vladimir was here. She half wondered if he had already seen Caleb and spoke to him, perhaps even hurt him. She held her tongue not wanting to ask, she didn't want to care about Caleb; she didn't want to know where he was. If he wanted to see her then he should be the one to come and see her.

Vladimir moved over towards her a sigh graced his lips and the bed began to press down and he was now sitting beside her. They both sat for a moment in silence, neither one saying anything before Vladimir looked up at her. "I believe I need to tell you something. Now before I do – please do let me finish the full story and then you can ask as many question as you like or do anything you like" Alexis found herself sitting up in curiosity.

What was so important that he had waited this long to tell her? So many questions and thoughts already began to stream through her mind about what he was going to say before he actually said it. *Was he going to tell her some lost story about why Caleb's temper was the way it was? Was he going to defend him?* Alexis had been trying to defend him in her own head and it wasn't working. She hoped that Vladimir would give her a reason to defend him.

Alexis nodded her head in agreement not having the strength to open her mouth and speak just in case all the questions came flooding from her mouth. Vladimir watched her for a moment as if trying to assess how she was going to react to what he was going to tell her.

There was no way he could guess, he had tried to so many times to tell her and every single time he had he had lost the courage but he couldn't do that now. She had already been hurt too much. She had already begun to lose too much.

The only way to get her wolf back was to tell her the truth and that was what she needed. She needed her wolf whether she liked to believe so or not. With a small deep unneeded breath in he was ready to begin his story. "Everything that you have been told since you got here has been a lie" That was his first sentence and while she digested it he kept silent before continuing on. "When Daniel brought you here all those long years ago it wasn't because your family had tried to kill everyone and was after you. In fact it was the complete opposite. Your family, your breed of werewolves were special. They're Royals that is why all the werewolves in the local area are attracted towards you. They can feel your leadership even above their own alphas" The room seemed to be getting smaller. Everything Vladimir was saying was making her world spin.

They had lied to her. They had all lied to her.

She felt like floating off on a dream, she felt like disappearing in her own head but she couldn't do that. She needed to hear this story. "They were called the Lupei. The Vampires, all of us were ordered to wipe out the Lupei bred by Daniel, Elizabeth and Leonardo. It was the first time the three had stood together in war. Everyone obeyed and slowly the Lupei werewolves were killed off. Till there was one left. The alpha pack – your pack" Alexis wanted to speak, her mouth even opened to do so. But she held back the words; she couldn't risk saying anything until she had heard the full story.

After all, she didn't know whether things were about to get better or worse. Her lips twitched and her eyes felt like they were filling with water.

"Daniel wanted to take it by force and he gathered everyone to attack, the day furthest away from the full moon of the month – Lupei wolves gathering their power from the moon. Lupei werewolves were normally born with a power especially the alpha family of the pack. They never expected it. The full pack was destroyed in a few hours apart from one little girl. The Alpha's wife had died in child birth not moments before the attack and a group had headed straight for the Alpha who was protecting his house, grief striking he had no chance against the vampires. That was your house. They killed your family but when it came to you, Daniel didn't kill you. Daniel found you, and kept you hidden until the fight was over and against Leonardo's judgement they came up with a plan. You're real name is Levesque, Alexis Levesque, although Daniel changed it in order to keep you from finding out and from any other wolves from finding you" Alexis was on the edge of her seat listening to the story. It was like her life was flashing through her eyes. S

he could never remember her childhood. She must have buried it in herself conscious and with what Vladimir was telling her there was no wonder. "They wanted to use werewolves to their advantage. It would have caused too much chaos if they had tried to kill every breed off but if they learned how to control them – Daniel thought it was the key to their control" Vladimir had turned away from Alexis and was staring off into the distance. He didn't want to see her face as he told the story. He knew it would be heart breaking to know his kind had killed off everyone she was supposed to love and then they had lied to her growing up. It wasn't going to be easy for her to take in.

With a deep breath he continued his story, trying to keep his voice from shaking. "He believed you were the key to their control. Louie and I were supposed to bring out your wolf and learn how to control it. It was about gaining your trust and taming your wolf. Daniel couldn't have guessed you would supress your werewolf gene – That was why he had so many regular visits" Alexis again opened her mouth to speak, her head tumbling with thoughts. She had been lied too, kept against her will - although she hadn't thought it was against her will- and brought up by the people who had killed her family.

Had Vladimir had something to do with that? Had he marched against her birth family?

The way he spoke was as if he wasn't there although at the beginning it had been as if he was. But how could she trust him? He had lied to her. "There had been no success and I refused to push you as far as the other elders wanted to. That was why Caleb was introduced. Like me, he is a child of Daniel and he has taken to Vampire-hood very well apart from his temper. Daniel thought his temper would be good against you hoping that he would break as he has done in the past and hoping that it would react in your wolf and bring her out. Which it has not" Vladimir stated the obvious although couldn't bring himself to look around at Alexis. She was like a daughter to him and he couldn't believe that he had lied to her all this time.

When she arrived he had automatically taken a liking to her – something about Alexis reminded him of his sisters. "I know that there is no use in apologising now. It is far too far down the line but I have protected you as much as I can. I have fought for your side in each meeting and every time they requested that Elizabeth or Leonardo take over; I have interjected and made sure that you have stayed here" Vladimir nodded his head knowing that without losing her he had done as much as he could. If he had told her any earlier it would have been lost on her. She would have been too young; she would have tried to venture out by herself and ended up more hurt than good.

Now she was old enough to at least realize what was best for her. When Vladimir stopped talking, they both sat in silence. He was afraid to look up and see her reaction and she wasn't sure what to say. She was angry of course, but she couldn't shout at him. She couldn't find the right words to use. *What could she say to him?* He felt bad, yes but he had broken her trust, he had lied to her. She shouldn't want to make him feel better. Alexis couldn't help but feel like she should, he had been her father from a very young age, and he had protected her from many people.

He had protected her from vampires; he had given her what she wanted. Alexis had always got what she wanted; he had always pushed so that she could have that.

Even letting her go to school was something she wanted. *But how could she forgive him? How could she not?* Vladimir stared at her, waiting for her to speak, trying to give her time to speak. He didn't want to say a word in case she started shouting. She was thinking and he was giving her that time to think.

Alexis turned her eyes to look at him, filled with water she refused to let them break. She refused to cry. "I..." Alexis started and pulled her lips tight as she thought of what to say, of how to get the words out. "How..." She shook her head not wanting to know the answers to the questions that were forming in her head. They wouldn't make her feel any better.

Nothing would. But it was in the past. *If she kept holding this up would it always be on her mind? Could she let this go?* Alexis shook her head nothing made sense. She had been living her life as a lie, she had lost her family and she wasn't even able to grieve them. She had never thought they were worth grieving. Taking in a deep breath and swallowing the lump in her thought she said exactly what she needed to.

Exactly what she was feeling because no matter what happened, no matter what continued to happen there was only one answer she could give to him. Everything he said didn't change her life, it didn't affect her, the way she thought it would, it wouldn't change who she was, and it didn't change anything.

Vladimir and Louie were her family, they had protected her since she came in this house and now Vladimir was protecting her by telling her the truth. There was only one thing she could say to that.

"I forgive you"

30

Nothing can go right from here

"I forgive you Vlady. I could never hate you, you have looked after me so well. You are not like anyone else I have met. I would have hated living with any other vampire. You have looked after me. Even Louie has cared for me in his own way" Her words echoed in her head as she searched through each room in the house that she had grown up in. She had meant every word she had said to Vladimir, she had told the truth to him, he had sacrificed a great deal to tell her the truth and he was sure the Elders weren't going to be happy when they found out.

But right now – Alexis didn't care about that. She couldn't care about that, she needed to find Caleb. Caleb had to be around here somewhere. It hadn't been that long ago since Alexis had last seen him. She rushed through the house ducking in his room to check if he was there. "Caleb" she called out but yet received no answer. She couldn't go back now and ask Vladimir, she needed to do this herself. Alexis stopped for a moment; she took in a deep breath and listened.

This good sense of hearing had to be good for something she thought as she tried to concentrated all her senses to one. Listening.

Alexis had never used her abilities, she had always focused on blocking them out, and never had she asked them for help like she was right now. Alexis closed her eyes hopping that it would help her ears pick something up more.

There.

She heard it, at the front of the house; she could hear voices – raised. That couldn't be good. She couldn't make out the voices but for some reason, her soul was telling her it was Caleb and she followed her feeling towards it. Rushing, she found herself picking up her pace until she was standing at the door staring at the boys.

A vampire and a werewolf at each other's neck in discussion and not a friendly discussion at that.

Caleb was upset and scary - he didn't look himself at all. He had already thrown his temper towards Alexis not long before this and regretted it immensely. But now he felt like his anger was rightly placed against the other werewolf, he wasn't going to hold back this time. His eyes had darkened although he tried to keep calm, his fangs were out and his body was tensed up.

What made things worse was that the werewolf he was fighting was Nicolas. Nicolas was angry and he couldn't hide it; his fists were scrunched up, his stance was rigid and his breathing was becoming erratic. He was on the edge, Alexis began to panic.

She knew what came next - he was going to change. She wanted to back away but felt like she couldn't, she couldn't let them hurt each other. She gathered up her courage and took a few steps forward.

"Stop this" Alexis spoke clearly trying to keep her voice from wavering but they didn't even acknowledge her. There fight continued and Alexis tried to focus on what they were talking about especially since it was so heated and included two people she cared about. "......you know nothing you stupid wolf pup. You don't even know the fights between our kinds so don't pretend to understand your ancestor's efforts, baby Alpha" Caleb was seething; he was speaking through gritted teeth. Alexis had never asked how old Caleb was although she knew he couldn't be older than Vladimir.

That was evident in the way they acted with each other. Caleb although he could push his luck never pushed too far. He was most definitely older or at least stronger than Louie. Louie was scared of Caleb and although he talked big, he stayed clear of him. Nicolas didn't seem to have the same problem, he was pushing and it didn't look like it was helping the situation. Nicolas's laugh echoed through the room making Alexis hair stand on edge.

"Like you know any different. Your eyes are black and you have emotions for a werewolf...I'm pretty sure vampires that knew about the real history wouldn't be so stupid or so caring. So you know more than I do, that isn't going to change how I feel or how I react" smugly Nicolas answered, although he didn't let up on his defensive stance. Nicolas was young, he had barely made it in to adult hood yet, he was only in his last year of school but yet right now he stood and acted much older than he was.

The alpha pup was brave, just as much as he was foolish. Alexis had known both boys about the same amount of time and both were stubborn, both wouldn't give up, both were acting extremely stupid.

They were mortal enemies by blood - but yet they didn't particular care about that part. They were fighting over a girl, a girl that had told them both no.

A girl that they weren't even listening to right now, that they didn't even know was screaming at them right now.

"Caleb! Nico! Stop it"

Alexis moved closer to them, they both still ignored her. "You're telling me how I feel? That's rich. Your fighting for a girl you don't even know who you have only just met, who doesn't even want to be a werewolf" Caleb was almost growling back at the werewolf, his anger growing by the moment, he could see Nicolas's wolf rising and he wanted it too. He knew that harming him would most likely hurt Alexis but right now it seemed worth it, it meant he wouldn't be in her life any more. "Only because of what you have told her. She's scared to be herself" Nicolas throw his hands up in the sir in frustration, he was angry at the fact that Alexis was scared of her wolf, she had buried it completely.

Neither Caleb nor Nicolas knew the real reason of why she had hide the wolf although they played against it. They both hadn't been around her over her younger years. "That cannot be blamed on vampires. They do not want her werewolf hidden and they have been trying countlessly to get it back out" The words they spoke were only encouraging them to fight more. They were moving daringly close to one another although not touching just yet. “Not for the right reasons I am sure. You want the wolf as a weapon” Nicolas spoke although not very kindly, his words spat out of his mouth as if they were trying to hold more force between them.

Caleb took a daring step forward putting his hands on Nicolas shoulders, which made him, growl from the back of his throat. ”Be very careful pup. You have no idea who you are messing with. Don't start something you can't finish" Caleb still spoke through gritted teeth, his head was lowered and he wore a dangerous glint that could almost be misinterpreted for a smile.

Alexis's own frustration was boiling, they weren't listening to her, and *did they even know she was in the same room as them?* They seemed oblivious. They were both so caught up in each other they hadn't acknowledged that someone else came in the room, they were blinded by rage and that seemed to block both of their good eye sites. Alexis looked to the door although their bickering hasn't alerted either Louie or Vladimir. She switched her eyes back to the boys and Nicolas's eyes had changed. The wolf in him was close to the surface. His hands were holding

Caleb's shoulders and one foot was placed in front of the other. "No. you don't know who your messing with night walker" Alexis had had enough, her own growl of frustration came through her mouth as she marched determinedly towards them. She stopped just short of where they were fighting, close enough to touch but again they didn't seem to see her.

It was if she wasn't even there. She reached forward to put her hand between them and on both of their arms. Without even acknowledging whom it was they both flung their hands sideways, their eyes never leaving each other. Their joint strength sent Alexa's flying back, her mouth opened in a scream yet she couldn't voice it. She flew through the air which to her, seemed in slow motion, they boys in front of her getting further and further away without turning towards her.

They didn't even know who they had hurt. All at once everything seemed to speed up, Alexa's back hut into the wall, she flinched in pain, she bounced slightly off the wall and crashed into the table below, her eyes scrunched up and her mouth closed tight, her body ached and felt heavy. She felt weak, she didn't even attempt to stand, her body was pushed up into a half seated position and she managed to push her eyes open slightly. She raised her hand to her head, trying to control the dizziness which was spreading fast against her eyes. She tried to position herself differently and let out a cry. She couldn't do that - her hand moved away from her head towards her side, it was sticky and wet; she pulled her hand out to see...blood.

Sickly sweet and dark red, it looked like it was a lot. Her hand had come away covered. Finally the boys turned, the smell of the blood catching both of their attention. Caleb's eyes still head their pure blackness- he looked stunned and at a loss, he hadn't seen her there. He couldn't remember her entering.

Nicolas gasped and pulled in a breath before rushing towards her "Lex" his voice was full of regret and he grabbed her hand away from her side trying to get a better look at what they had done. He could hardly see the damage for the blood.

It was streaming out. Caleb had moved with speed to her opposite side and handed Nicolas the cover from the table she had landed on to press against her wound without looking towards him. Caleb's eyes found hers and he gripped her face. "Alexis you will be fine. Keep looking at me, don't lose conscience" Caleb tried to keep his attention on her, her blood was so sweet and tempting and as much as he hated to admit it, it did tempt him. He would have loved nothing more than to enjoy that temptation like he had always been taught to do.

He shook his head away from those thoughts. "How bad is it?" Caleb asked trying not to make his voice waver while he spoke. When Nicolas didn't answer his head turned towards him, Nicolas shook his head and pushed the cloth into Alexis's hip where something had lodged itself there. Alexis's let out a squeal and shut her eyes.

The pain was blinding and she tried to keep up with their conversation but each time she thought she was getting away from the pain her eyes would start to drift closed. Her clothes were soaked with blood "She needs medical attention and not human, nor vampire medics can help. Her blood will only get sweeter the more it drains out her side. Your people wouldn't be able to help her. We need to take her to my pack" Nicolas knew that the vampire wasn't going to like that idea and by the face he pulled Nicolas was right.

Caleb turned his head away from both of them; Daniel would more than likely kill him if he let the Lupei werewolf go especially to other werewolves. His mind was having trouble digesting every bit of information. He also knew Nicolas was correct - she wouldn't live if she stayed here or if the vampires tried to help her. Caleb was finding it difficult to concentrate with the blood he doubted any other vampire would be much different.

"We don't have much time Caleb" Nicolas snapped trying to grab the vampires' attention. Caleb's head nodded and he moved himself closer to Alexis. "Fine. But I will take her with you. I am not leaving her side until she asks me too" Caleb was already going to be in trouble with his elders so there wasn't much point in backing away now. He was going to protect *his* werewolf no matter what. Nicolas fought with the idea in his head knowing that bring a vampire into his pack lands wasn't going to go down well.

Alexis whimpered losing herself to the blood lose. Her eyes closed and her body started to loosen. That made the decision for him. Caleb was coming. "Agreed" he spoke through gritted teeth as Caleb swung his arms under Alexis and pulled her up into his body tightly.

Nicolas held back his temper of a vampire holding his mate, his head nodded and he turned to head out the door, Caleb following closely on his heel. "Stay with us Alexis" Caleb whispered towards her before her body went completely limp in his arms.

31

She's out

Alexis's head was rough, she could feel something banging on her temple but yet she couldn't tell what it was. Her body felt numb, she pulled her hands into fists to make sure she could still move and she wiggled her toes. They were all still working but yet her body still felt numb. Her eyes opened to a pure white ceiling. She blinked a few times before turning her head to the side. The room was clean and bright, it all seemed too clean, too bright. It hurt her eyes.

Alexis turned her head back to look at the ceiling. *Where was she?* She couldn't remember what happened. She tried to push herself up in a sitting position and her hands moved to her side lifting her T-shirt. It was covered in a white bandage; she poked and prodded at it for a moment, trying to remember what happened. She winced. She hurt herself; she was obviously damaged under the bandage. She couldn't…..She could remember what happened.

The boys – *her* boys were fighting, she had tried to get through to them and yet nothing had seemed to grab their attention away from their argument. When she had moved closer, they had lashed out at each other and she had got caught into it. She must have hurt herself worse than she thought when she fell. She could remember Caleb and Nicolas fighting and bickering.

They were discussing something although she couldn't remember what. She pulled herself up straighter so that her back was straight against the back frame of the bed. Her mouth was dry and her stomach gurgled with hunger. She felt like she hadn't eaten or drunk anything in a week. She pushed her feet out of the bed and pressed them on to the carpet.

It felt good against her skin, she stretched out her feet and she could feel the beginnings of cramp, she had been lying down for a while. She pressed herself on to her feet – testing to see if her feet could take her weight. She was a little bit wobbly but it didn't take her long to feel the strength returning to her legs. She stumbled away from the bed making sure to try and keep her balance, she moved into the bathroom and cleaned herself up, her face felt dry and her throat was bare. She moved out of the bathroom and towards the little kitchen area where she could see some water in a jug. "Well look who's up and about" the deep voice came from behind her; she tried to turn and winced. Her side wouldn't allow her to move that fast. Caleb who was once sitting on her bed was now beside her in a flash. His hands placed around her and ushered her to the small couch in the room, he tried to take most of the weight from her.

"Please don't hurt yourself. You've been knocked out enough" Caleb's face looked pained and he sat down beside her. Alexis smiled towards him "I'm so glad to see you're okay" She moved to hug him and his body chuckled, she could feel it vibrate through her although she still hugged him tight. She felt like she hadn't seen him in so long – he was still here and she hadn't thought he would be. She didn't even know where she was. "I am perfectly fine Alexis. It is you that has had everybody worried to death. You have been knocked out for a week. Your wounds were so bad they had to give you countless numbers of drugs while they attended to you. They wouldn't let me in until they were finished they were too scared that I would be too attracted to your blood" Caleb's head lowered and he looked like he felt guilty that he wasn't able to help in any way.

Alexis put her hands on his and rubbed them slightly. She didn't want him to worry. If he could have been there then she knew he would have. He had done so much for her and although he had a temper she was sure he could get by it. "I understand Cal. It's fine. Don't worry about it" She tried to reassure him with a small smile. She squeezed his hands another time, her full body felt on edge for some reason.

The hairs on her body stood on edge and she shivered slightly. "What's wrong?" Caleb's eyes furrowed, he could feel her body reacting, he could feel her body tensing up. Alexis couldn't control what was happening to her, it was like the heat from her body was bursting from her. "I'm not sure" she shook her head, she couldn't be changing, Vladimir had told her countless numbers of times that she would know what it was like to change when it happened. She would be able to tell right away and she knew she would fight it away.

"Are you changing?" Caleb's eyes widened and she felt him tense up. Vampires and Werewolves didn't have a good relationship as it was and although Alexis might not hurt him, he wasn't so sure that the wolf in her would give him the same luxury. "It's because her wolf senses she's near a werewolf pack. We are pack animals after all" Nicolas spoke at the entrance to the small room – she could tell it was him without even looking.

Another reason he *knew* she was his mate although she denied it. She still couldn't feel the same things that he did. She had closed her wolf away, locked it up and although she felt attracted to him, she didn't feel the bond that he felt. Alexis turned around, her eyes looking up to Nicolas – he was still so beautiful. He had obviously just been for a shower, his hair was still wet and he had new clothes on, less clothes on than he usually had.

A tank top showed off his muscles and she couldn't believe the reaction her body was given to him. She tried to push it down. She refused to act on her feelings no matter what he said. She wouldn't choose between Caleb and Nicolas; they could both be her friends and find happiness elsewhere. She didn't want to hurt either of them.

So she could only hurt herself this way. She wouldn't pick. "We are at your pack?" Alexis questioned him – Nicolas and Caleb shared a look before he answered. "What do you remember?" he moved closer to the two on the couch and Alexis moved closer to Caleb to make space for him although he didn't sit down. She frown "I remember you two fighting and I was trying to get your attention and snap you out of it but I couldn't. I tried to touch you to snap you out of it and then I was flying through the air and then nothing" Alexis tried to remember everything she could although it all seemed out of her touch, it was like she was living a dream and not life itself.

She was watching herself fly through the room as if she was watching it from the outside, she shook her head to try and get rid of the thoughts and concentrate on the present situation. "You were flung back into the wall and crashed into one of Vladimir's tables. The table collapsed and you ended up with some of it in your side" Caleb spoke grabbing her attention and trying to bring some clarity to the situation. "You couldn't go to the hospital as well you probably know because of your werewolf gene. So we brought you to the pack healer, Caleb insisted he come with you and well we had no other choice. I have vouched for him at the moment" Nicolas's eyes stared at Caleb for a moment before returning them warmly to Alexis.

Alexis flinched slightly, that couldn't be good – she had put two enemies in a room together and made them behave, she had also put Caleb in a very dangerous situation. She was making him stay with a pack of werewolves.

That couldn't have been good.

Alexis shook off the thought and stood to her feet in front of the boys. “Right well I’m all better now. We can leave, then there will be no trouble with your kinds” Alexis smiled towards both of them although they didn’t share the smile. Caleb knew she wasn’t about to like what she was about to be told, he knew she would fight against them and that was why for the second time Nicolas and him would have to work together to make her understand. They had to be on the same page which they weren’t often.

“Our kinds” Nicolas couldn’t help but add in stubbornly, his arms folded on his chest and Caleb shook his head resting the urge to punch the werewolf. This was going to be a difficult situation enough without the pup making it worse. “Nicolas” Caleb shot him a look which only made the werewolf roll his eyes. Alexis’s eyebrows furrowed and she watched them bicker, she could tell something was up. They were normally at each other’s throats, not like this.

This was different. “We have both been talking Alexis and we feel like you’d be much better here. You’ve been away from

Vladimir's house for a week now and Daniel will start to suspect something about where you have been when I get back." Alexis's mouth opened slightly trying to think of words to protest, they couldn't do this too her. She couldn't live with werewolves. She hadn't ever changed into one and she wasn't every going to. *They both expected her to live here, to make this her home?* "But…." Alexis started to speak but was interrupted with Nicolas this time "Caleb's right. As much as I hate to agree with him. You belong here. You are one of us and right now it's the safest place for you especially since you're the last Lupei werewolf" he was being stern and that couldn't help but bring out Alexis's stubborn side.

Caleb could see it coming out as well; he stood up and gripped on to her arms making her look at him. "You need to stay here Alexis. It's important. Daniel won't let you disappear so easily. Especially since he has worked so hard on you. It's no secret in the vampire world that he had a werewolf project" Caleb tried to make her see sense, her shoulders dropped and she nodded her head. She couldn't fight against the vampires especially since she wouldn't accept her werewolf side.

"Do you have to leave?" Alexis stared at Caleb; they couldn't make her change if she still had a vampire nearby on her side. Not that she thought Nicolas wasn't on her side; he had always given her hope and made her see another side.

Nicolas couldn't help but flinch when he heard her words, she spoke to Caleb with care and even though she spoke to him the same, it would always hurt when she showed that *leech* affection in front of him. She was worried and scared still – Nicolas could see that, his eyes looked to the ground and Caleb couldn't help but look at Nicolas and notice his discomfort before looking at Alexis again to answer. "I can't stay in the pack. Your mobile is here though and you can get a hold of me at any time. I will be close by I promise and right now I will stay until you feel better" Caleb looked again to Nicolas to check that wasn't going to affect anything but the werewolf's head was still lowered and he wouldn't look back at him.

Alexis followed his eyes and noticed how uncomfortable Nicolas was – she let go of her grip on Caleb and took a step backwards. "Thank you" She answered softly.

"Both of you" She shared her look with Nicolas and Caleb trying to lighten the situation again. Nicolas smiled a little bit towards her – although she could still feel his nervousness. Alexis flinched, her hands moving straight to her side, Nicolas and Caleb automatically forgot about the earlier situation and rushed to her side just as her legs began to wobbly. Her side was beginning to ache. The pain was beginning to return. "You need to lie down and rest, your body hasn't completely healed yet. It would have been much easier if you had your wolf on your side. You need to let her out, you will heal much faster if you do" She could hear Nicolas's voice in the distance but it was as if it was getting further away. She shook her head – she understood what he was saying and she couldn't let her out. She wouldn't let her out. Alexis could feel strong hands grip her and move her about the room and lay her down on her bed.

Her head was shaking constantly, she couldn't, and it was too dangerous.

She could no longer see, everything was blurred. "Alexis listen to him. Let your wolf help you, let her heal you" Caleb's voice was distant although soft and caring and she couldn't help but smile. "She needs more medication" She also heard him snap towards Nicolas and she heard him answer back although she couldn't make out the whispered words. Not completely anyway. "We wouldn't be having this problem if her wolf was out" louder this time, Alexis heard every word. She frowned, the pain was unbearable and now both her boys were telling her it would be fixed and she would live with her wolf. Had she been scared of her wolf for nothing? No that couldn't be true…

"Let her in Lex" Nicolas words were becoming further away still, she felt as if he was speaking to her from a distance. It had to be right if they were both saying it, didn't there. She could feel no jab of pain medication, so all she was feeling was purely from the pain. She could hear them mumbling more words but couldn't make out what they were saying anymore.

They both thought the solution was her wolf so there had to be some truth in it.

These past few weeks with Nicolas had proved to her that not all wolves were bad – she had touched his wolf and it had been soft and gentle. *So maybe there was something?* Maybe her wolf was safe. There was only one way to find out. *But where to start?* Alexis began to focus away from the world and concentrated on finding her wolf. She dug through her own mind wondering where she had hide it all those years ago, she had been a little girl scared of all those stories, Vladimir and Louie had told her.

"Hello" Alexis spoke hearing it echo around herself. She felt like she was running in circles and yet it was never ending. There was no place to turn; there was no place to stop, there was nothing. How was she ever going to find her wolf? Nicolas had once called her wolf something; if he was her mate then the wolf would have to react to that word. It was worth a shot. Everything was. *"Lupus"* Alexis called out as she circled herself. She heard a growl and her full body tensed in

anticipation, had she fallen into one of her nightmares? She couldn't remember. All her thoughts drained away.

She was supposed to be looking for her wolf. Was that all a charade? Was this just her head playing tricks on her? *"No. It is me Alexis. You've had me locked up in here for a very long time. I didn't think I was ever going to hear your voice again"* Alexis could hear the voice although she couldn't see the source yet. It felt like it was coming from everywhere yet at the same time nowhere. *"I'm sorry, Lupus. I didn't know what to do. I didn't know what you were. I thought you were dangerous. I thought you would get us both killed"* Alexis answered her wolf in worry and she heard it chuckle. *"We are dangerous, of course. We are a werewolf but not in the way you have been told. You have been misinformed of our nature. We are the last of the Lupei Werewolf. You are the last of us. In order for us to proceed as a species you have to mate. Otherwise all will be lost"* The werewolf's voice was sweet and soft, it trickled around her and licked the tip of her ears as it spoke.

"Mate? You mean Nicolas?" Alexis spoke, although scared of the answer, she couldn't pick between them. She wouldn't let herself or her wolf pick. The wolf chuckled again. *"We are not ready to pick a mate, I see that. We can take it one step at a time. We don't age like others. We will be strong for a while yet. Are you going to let me out?"* The wolf purred and Alexis turned trying to see where the voice was coming from. Alexis knew her wolf wanted out, she had dreamt about it, she had heard that she wanted out, she had felt her scrapping at the back of her mind but she had always ignored it. She had always hid it.

Now was a different time, now she was ready to answer her. *"What do I have to do?"* Alexis didn't need to sigh in defeat because she hadn't given in, she hadn't betrayed herself in any way and she wouldn't do anything she didn't want to. She was joining forces with her wolf. She didn't seem that bad after all. She understood what Alexis wanted. She was more confident and out spoke than Alexis but she understood her.

Alexis was sure she could handle someone else in her mind. She was sure that this wolf would be a help to her. She could hear her wolf smile. *"Let me in. Focus on a door in your mind and open it. Forget about ever closing me out and wake up. I will take care of the rest"* Her wolf was gentle and sweet, she nodded her head and closed her eyes. She began to envision the door just like her wolf had told her too.

Alexis couldn't help but imagine a big grand door with stone pillars as if it had jumped straight out from a castle scene. She imagined herself pushing it open with all her force, struggling for a little while before she was finally able to gain access and a bright light began to appear through it. Alexis shield her eyes before it over took all her thoughts and she plummeted in to darkness. Her body felt on fire, she could feel the bed sheets underneath her again and she gripped onto them. She was alive, she was in reality. She fought to open her eyes and struggled to sit up. Her body felt better, a bit sore and strained in places but the pain that was once there was gone.

Was that her wolf? Had she helped? Her eyes focused on Caleb and Nicolas sitting curiously in front of her, worried to death. They looked tired. *How long had she been out for this time?* "Are you ….you're eyes." Caleb gasped squinting towards Alexis. She could hear a growl before she realised it was coming from within herself. Nicolas stared in amazement at her eyes that were now light blue almost white, her pupil were tiny. "Your wolf, Alex" his voice was soft and in awe. Alexis smiled, or was that her wolf? She could feel something wriggling through her skin and settling in as if it was right at home.

"That's more like it. Now let's take a different approach"

Epilogue

Nicolas ushered Alexis along towards the meeting, pulling on her arm. He had a smile on his face. "We need to hurry before it starts" Nicolas grinned back towards her. Alexis tried to quicken her pace but her bones were still aching, they all hurt – they had all started to hurt since she had changed into a wolf on a regular basis. *"This wouldn't be happening if you had let us change a lot sooner. You're body isn't used to changing at all and now we need to make it get used to it"* Alexis's eyes rolled slightly "Yeah okay wolfie" She mumbled under her breath and Nicolas through another smile her way.

Every time she had a conversation with her wolf, he watched on with a bright smile as if he were happy she were finally talking to her. Alexis still couldn't decide whether it had been a good idea or not. "Where are we going Nico?" Alexis asked her voice turning into a whine. She didn't want to be in the Alpha's house. She hated being here, between Nicolas's brothers poking and prodding at her and his father watching over her and talking to her like a child – she couldn't decide which was worse.

Not that she had gotten used to living in the pack – she had been here 2 months now and she missed both Vladimir and Louie terribly.

She wasn't given a chance to miss Caleb considering he met her at the gates every couple of weeks, much too Nicolas's disagreement. Nicolas stopped at a door. "You need to be completely silent in here. My dad it only letting us in on that condition" Nicolas pushed his finger to his lips before he moved through the door and Alexis followed suit slipping into the chair beside him once he was seated down.

The room was packed with elder men and Nicolas's brothers. Nicolas's dad sat at the head table with his beta behind him – he was a scary bald man that had seen better days, Alexis was sure. *"He's a beta what do you expect? You've met Alexander. It's a trait the beta's have"* Her wolf chimed in on her thoughts causing Alexis to growl slightly.

Nicolas slid his gaze sideways asking her if she was okay and Alexis nodded her head. The room was mostly full of men with just three women sitting down, one of which was pregnant. "Are you sure of this information?" Nicolas's dad, Axel inquired towards the wolf in front of him.

The wolf had long black hair and was down on one knee. "I am positive. He has been hopping pack's since he was a child. Apparently he is looking for his mate in order to continue the line" The wolf spoke softly but clearly and left no questions to be answered when the alpha spoke. Axel sat back in his chair for a moment, pondering his thoughts. "How sure are you he is a Lupei?" Axel asked and both Alexis and her wolf perked up sliding their gaze towards Nicolas who held his finger next to his mouth again before pointing back to his father. *"It's not possible"* her wolf whispered although Alexis was trying to listen to the conversation in front of her.

"There is no doubt. At first they thought he was a rogue Farkas but he has authority that no other pack member can have. Once he has seen every member of the pack he backs away and leaves" the wolf continued on.

Axel seemed to consider what he was saying for a moment.

His head bounced into a nod as if he were agreeing to something within his head. "We need to get a hold of him then. Help him out and make sure he is safe. If he's moving around packs then he obviously found where he belongs and thinks he is unsafe" Axel's words left no room for question and everyone nodded in agreement. "What's his name?" Axel inquired towards the wolf, leaning forward he came closer to the edge of the table. "Dominick Levesque"

"Levesque!" her wolf echoed out and Alexis squinted down towards her hands. *Why did she recognise that name?* It was so familiar. Gasps surrounded the room pulling her away from her

thoughts before she got a chance to come up with anything. She hushed her wolf so that she could hear what was happening. “Shut up” She whispered when the wolf wouldn’t listen to what she was saying. “He’s an Alpha then. That makes him more important. If he’s the Alpha of the Alpha race he obviously has the ability” one of the other wolves around the room spoke causing Alexis’s head to turn for a moment. *He was the alpha of her species?*

She couldn’t think if that was good or bad. It meant he could have control over her like no other wolf could. That didn’t sound good in theory. Her wolf growled in her head. *“He has no control over us”* it answered and she couldn’t help but want to question what she meant. *“Levesque! Don’t you recognise the name?”* The wolf spoke with a smile to his lips and Alexis shook her head not wanting to speak in this seemingly silent room. *“He’s you’re brother. Your name is Alexis Levesque”* “You have got to be kidding me” Alexis spoke out loud causing eyes to cast towards her.

Alexis blushed slightly, wishing to curl up in a ball and disappear. "Alexis?" Nicolas spoke softly and Alexis stood to her feet and smiled apologetically towards the older wolves in the room before she rushed out of the room. *"What are you running from?"* The wolf inquired and she shook her head partly because she didn't know what she was running from and neither did she know what she wanted to do. "I need air" she answered her wolf instead as she moved along the corridors until she made her way outside.

The Alpha house was always so claustrophobic and right now it seemed worse. Everything was coming in on her. Her brother? She had family? He was alive. How is that even possible? *"People thought the same for you, perhaps he was saved by someone"* the wolf tried to ease her thoughts but they couldn't be eased. She shook her head again and pulled her hands up to her head; she covered it and put her back to the wall of the house. *"You know I'm right!"* the wolf persisted and Alexis groaned inwardly at its voice in her head. She couldn't think straight. She was so used to being in her own head, by herself, that this was beginning to give her a headache.

"We need to find him, pup! He's our shot at family. You won't accept your mate, but you have to accept your brother. We need to go and get him. Now!" the wolf's words grilled her and although she knew it was true, she also wanted to find her brother. She just needed to breathe right now. She just wanted two seconds to catch her breath and believe that her whole life hadn't been a lie. She wanted to go back to Cassie and be a normal human girl. She wanted to pretend that Vladimir wasn't a vampire and he was just her over protective dad. She could pretend that Louie was the weird uncle and that Caleb was a friend.

She slipped down till she was sitting on the ground. "Shut up" She shouted towards her wolf who stayed silent with her words, the wolf had learned to push her so far before being silent. They had an understanding that sometimes Alexis needed to be within her own head by herself and although it was impossible now the wolf tried her best to find a way to do it.

“Alexis” the familiar voice was in front of her again and she looked through her arms to see Nicolas in front of her. He was on his knees and his hands were hovering beside her. They were aching to touch her but again he held back, he had held back a lot over the past 2 months which Alexis was surprised at. “What’s the matter?” Nicolas asked concern lacing his voice; Alexis stared towards Nicolas in wonder. Did he not know? None of them knew her second name.

None of them knew how important this situation really was. She needed to find that wolf. She needed to find her family. There was no other option. “Dominick’s my brother. My name is Alexandra Levesque” Alexis stated causing Nicolas to bounce back on his feet. Silence filled the air before anything else was said.

“I didn’t see that one coming” Nicolas ran his hand over his face, shaking his head. “We better tell my father”